LIAM

AN EIDOLON BLACK OPS NOVEL: BOOK 4

MADDIE WADE

Liam
An Eidolon Black Ops Novel: Book 4
by Maddie Wade
Published by Maddie Wade
Copyright © May 2020 Maddie Wade

Cover: Envy Creative Designs
Editing: Black Opal Editing
Formatting: Black Opal Editing

COPYRIGHT

ACKNOWLEDGMENTS

I am so lucky to have such an amazing team around me without which I could never bring these books to life. I am so grateful to have you in my life, you are more than friends you are so essential to my life. Writing is a solitary job unless you have people who share your passion. Many times I have called on one of you when I have written myself into a corner and with a few words you allow me to see the bigger picture and find the answers I need.

My wonderful beta team, Greta, and Deanna who are brutally honest and beautifully kind. If it is rubbish you tell me it is and if you love it you are effusive. Your support means so much to me.

To the ladies of Words Whiskey and Wine for Woman, you are my crew and I love you.

My editor—Linda at Black Opal Editing, I have, and still learn, so much from you. You are more than editor; you are a good friend.

Thank you to my group Maddie's Minxes. Your support and love for Fortis, Eidolon, and all the books I write is so important to me. Special thanks to Rowena, Tracey, Faith, Rachel, Carolyn, Kellie, Maria, Greta, Deanna, Rihaneh and Linda L for making the group such a friendly place to be.

My ARC Team for not keeping me on edge to long while I wait for feedback.

Lastly and most importantly thank you to my readers who have embraced my books so wholeheartedly and shown a love for the stories in my head. To hear you say that you see my characters as family makes me so humble and proud. I hope you enjoy Liam and Taamira, he has waited a long time for his happy ever after.

DEDICATION

I am dedicating Liam to Linda. You teach me so much, are always there for me and you do it with calm. I didn't just find the best editor in the world I found an amazing friend.

PROLOGUE

HE STARED at the man in the long mirror, dressed in a black suit, black shirt, his regimental tie, the medals on his chest, their weight heavy. The Military Cross and the Victoria Cross among others more undeserved than ever. He sighed, pushing away the feelings and placed the sand-coloured beret on his head, then looked away, unable to face what he saw.

Liam looked just the same as he always had, but his eyes held a pain so deep it would never leave him. His best friend, the man he had grown up with, got into trouble with, joined the army with, and then followed into the Special Air Service was gone—dead. All because of a group who wanted destruction and hatred to rule the earth.

He strode from the room, down the stairs, and out of the front door. He looked to the heavens and noted the rain clouds moving across the sky. He tossed his head and strode to his car. He would not be late for Ambrose; he would not let him down again—but that was because he would never get the chance.

Crippling grief stole through his body, and he fought the impact as if it were a physical blow. Fifteen minutes, that was all it had been, but he'd arrived too late to save his friend from the attack which had eventually taken his life. Stealing his life force, taking Ambrose's soul one piece at a time as he faded away until he was gone. No longer of this earth, no more would he be beside Liam on a mission.

Never again would he hold his son and turn his smile of affection on the woman he loved. Natai would grow up without a father, but Liam would make sure he knew him. He would make sure he wanted for nothing that was in his power to give him. Liam just mourned that it would never be Ambrose doing that for his son.

He would give his own life in a heartbeat if he thought it would bring his friend—no, his brother—back but it couldn't. So, as he pulled up outside the home where Ambrose had lived with his small family, he vowed he would do whatever he could the make the blow Ambrose's son had been dealt a little less painful.

He glanced up as he climbed the steps to the front door and saw Gail standing in the doorway. She wore a long, black belted dress, black heels, and dark coat, her face pale and already tearstained before the day began.

"Hi, sweetheart," Liam said as he came to a stop in front of her, leaning in to kiss her cheek. She turned empty, watery eyes on him before she spun without comment and walked back into the house. Liam hated the pain he saw in her eyes. Gail was normally so full of life, laughing and dancing with Ambrose in the kitchen.

He'd never seen a couple laugh so much together; they had been a match made in heaven. Her fire and his calm, the love they had for each other could be seen in every smile or look. Liam had envied them in some ways, wanting that for himself, yet he never begrudged either of them. They made him a part of their family. Gail had never wanted to come between the friends and accepted Liam as part of Ambrose.

Liam loved her almost as much as he knew his friend had but in a very different way. Gail was the sister he'd never had, so to see her so broken up over the loss of a man such as Ambrose was gut-wrenching.

"Uncle Liam."

Liam looked towards the stairs and saw Natai at the top watching him. At three years old, he was the spitting image of his father. Liam saw so much of his friend in the boy it caused his chest to ache.

"Hey, little man." Liam held out his arms to his godson, and the boy raced into them, jumping the last step so Liam caught him. "Wow, you're getting so big, I won't be able to catch you much longer."

Natai regarded him seriously, his big brown eyes so full of sadness Liam almost sagged under the weight of it. "Mummy is sad."

Liam's chest ached where his heart beat an unsteady tattoo, but he had to ignore his pain and do what was necessary for this innocent child. Bending, he sat on the bottom step, the boy on his knee, as he heard the sobs from the living room, followed by a murmur of voices which he couldn't face.

Twisting, he faced Natai. "Mummy misses Daddy, and that makes her sad," he explained, not knowing how much to tell him.

"Why doesn't Daddy come home then?"

The question asked by the child had him wanting to weep. He clenched his fist to try and control his own emotion as he swallowed. "Because Daddy had to go to heaven where he could help all the other angels fight for the good people here."

Natai angled his head as he chewed his lip. "Like Thor?"

Liam fought the grin that was suddenly on his lips at the thought of his friend dressed as Thor. "Not quite but it does mean you won't see Daddy anymore and neither will Mummy, and that's why she's sad."

"Are you sad, Uncle Liam?"

God, this kid was killing him, making him want to lie on the floor and cry like a baby. "I'm very sad."

"Me too. I don't want Daddy to be an angel." He laid his head on Liam's chest. "I want him to play cars with me."

"I'll play cars with you, buddy."

"Okay, Uncle Liam."

He heard the resigned tone in his voice, it wasn't the same as Ambrose doing it, and they both knew it.

Gail walked out from the room and peered at them with grief etched into her expression. "The car is here."

She held her arms out for her son, and Liam stood and handed Natai to his mother who held on as if the child was the only thing keeping her breathing, and perhaps he was.

He opened the door and let Gail and Natai proceed him as the hearse carrying his best friend's body drew up to the curb. A tight band of pain squeezed his chest and nausea swam in his belly as he saw the flowers covering the coffin. Son, Daddy, Ambrose, and their regimental insignia all made up in flowers so barely any wood showed.

It slowed to a stop, and he helped Gail and Natai into the car behind the hearse and climbed in after them. Her family would follow and so would Ambrose's mother and father, his sisters, and their families.

He stared out of the window lost in his thoughts over the next few minutes as they drove to the church where a majority of SAS soldiers found their final resting place. He alighted the vehicle and helped Gail out, keeping his hand on her back for support.

He saw his friends from Fortis, his colleagues from Eidolon— Jack, Lopez, Reid, Blake, Waggs, Mitch, Alex, and finally Decker. They stood with their heads bowed solemnly as they waited for Gail to go inside with Natai and her family.

He approached them then, and no words were needed as his friends squeezed his shoulder to offer their silent support or placed a hand on his back. Zack Cunningham offered his hand to shake, as did Dane, Daniel, Lucy, Nate.

He then stepped back and watched as the undertakers pulled the coffin from the back of the car.

Jack stepped close to him. "Are you ready?"

"No," Liam answered honestly.

The weight of Jack's hand on his shoulder was an anchor he

needed. "I know, brother, but let's give him the send-off he deserves. He lived a hero. He died a hero, and he'll remain a hero, always."

Liam nodded, not trusting his voice to speak.

They began to get in position, Liam and Jack at the front, Dane and Daniel in the middle, and Zack and Mitch at the back. The others would follow behind and take their seats.

As they hoisted their friend on to their shoulders and carried him inside to begin the service that would end with him committed into the ground, Liam struggled to catch his breath and knew he'd never breathe easy again.

The next hour was a blur as he kept his eyes on the mahogany coffin, not wanting to look away, knowing this was the last time his friend would be on this earth. He didn't feel the tears that fell silently down his face until Gail handed him a tissue.

With Ambrose committed into the ground, they made the short drive back to Gail's home where she was holding the wake. Liam grabbed a beer and moved to the back garden wanting some time to get his thoughts together.

He sat on the step, and a kaleidoscope of memories moved through his mind of time spent in this very place. Ambrose laughing and playing Nerf with his son, Ambrose getting pelted by snowballs as Gail and Natai hid behind the shed and ambushed him last winter. Ambrose and him as they built the swing set that now sat still.

He drank and remembered. He had no idea how long he sat there before a presence behind him had him turn, tipping his head back to see Mitch ambling towards him, his relaxed gait tensed for once.

"Mind if I sit?"

Liam lifted his chin in ascent.

The two men sat in silence for a while, and then Mitch spoke. "When I was sixteen, I lost my best friend to gang violence."

Liam twisted his head in surprise at the words. Mitch turned his almost coal-black eyes to Liam, and he saw the pain was still fresh.

"He was so smart, so alive, and we got caught up in a world we thought we could control. It was fun, we were clever, had money and standing in the community, and then we didn't. A rival gang wanted our turf, and it stopped being fun and clever. In one night, I lost my best friend and learned lessons no boy of sixteen should ever have to learn. My ma moved us away, and I knuckled down and worked hard to live a life worthy of him. To live for us both and do it in a way where he'd be proud of what I'd achieved. I pray every day that I'm doing that by saving others and giving back."

Mitch placed the empty bottle on the floor between his bent legs and glanced at him. "The pain never goes, it will always be a part of you. It will either bury you or it will make you strive to be the man he knew you were." Mitch stood then and put a hand on Liam's back. "I hope you choose the second one, my friend."

Liam didn't answer but he hoped so too, he just didn't know if he had it in him.

An hour later he heard a commotion and stood to see what was going on. He found Gail in the kitchen; she was with her sister and best friend, who looked at him with bewilderment as Gail cried and started throwing mugs.

"Get Natai upstairs," he commanded her sister who moved to do just that, leaving him and Gail alone as she continued to rant.

"Don't you take my son anywhere."

Liam moved to steady her as she swayed, and he realised she had been drinking.

"Take your fucking hands off me." The hate and venom had him pulling back as she glared at him with hatred in her face.

"Sweetheart, I'm not the enemy here," he said slowly, his heart beating fast.

"Yes, you are," she snarled. "If you had been there, he would be alive. Ambrose's death is your fault. You killed him."

Liam blanched at her words, almost an echo of his thoughts from that morning.

"My son is fatherless because of you. My Ambrose is dead because of you." She began to sob, and he approached, pulling her into his arms. She sagged and cried for a few minutes before she pushed him away with a heave. "Leave, get out. I never want to see you again, you murderer."

Liam stood frozen with anguish and pain at her words, at his loss. All of it too much, he turned and walked quickly for the door. He had lost more today than just Ambrose; he had lost his family.

Liam Hayes' heart hardened at that moment, but he vowed he would live a life that would make his friend proud, even if it killed him.

CHAPTER ONE

THE TENSION in the room was so thick, Liam could almost taste it. He stared at the man sitting on a lone chair in the middle of the room, his legs and hands restrained, a black bag made of harsh calico over his head. Jack and Alex on either side of him, along with Decker, a former FBI profiler, in the dark room that was Eidolon's interrogation area. Decker always took part in these 'interviews'.

This one though was different from any other interrogation he'd ever been part of, and he had conducted a lot in his time. All the men who worked for Eidolon had been through the extensive Resistance to Interrogation training, known as RTI, used by the SAS to train all of their recruits. The man in front of him was no different. What was unusual was that he'd once been a trusted member of the team.

Liam glanced at Jack, who nodded silently, giving Liam the signal to remove the cover from Gunner Ramberg's head. Liam controlled the mixture of anger, betrayal, and fury inside him as he watched Gunner blink as his eyes adjusted to the light in the room. As he did, Liam saw him look around at each of the men present, assessing them as he would do in the same position.

Finally, Gunner's gaze stopped on Jack as the leader of the team

—his old leader before he'd betrayed them. Liam clenched his fists in an effort to remain calm on the outside at least. What did surprise Liam was the lack of expression on Gunner's face. It wasn't what he was trying to hide that surprised Liam, but rather what he wasn't hiding.

He didn't show signs of hate or dislike. In fact, Liam could see he was trying hard not indicate anything, yet relief was in his every movement. This surprised Liam, and he looked at Decker, wondering what he thought. Of course, Decker didn't show a single emotion, the man was like a robot with the way he hid every personal feeling, as if worried someone would perhaps profile him.

Jack stepped forward his arms loose at his sides. "Nothing to say? No apology or excuses?" His voice was hard and cold, and Liam was glad he wasn't on the wrong side of that.

Gunner angled his head to look up at Jack. "Is there any point? You've already decided how you feel." Gunner shrugged, but it wasn't without feeling, it was resigned. "I don't blame you for hating me, fuck, I hate myself."

"I hope you don't expect us to feel sorry for you," Alex growled from where he leaned against the wall, his arms crossed.

Gunner twisted to him and shook his head. "No. But I'm praying with everything in me that you're better men than I am. That you're the men I know you to be."

Liam let out a bark of humourless laughter. "You don't know fuck about me."

Gunner focused on him. "Don't I? I know you still mourn Ambrose. That you always resented me for taking his spot on the team."

Liam dove for Gunner, his hand clamping around his throat as fury almost blinded him. "Don't speak his fucking name. You're not fit to lick his shoes. He was ten times the man you are, that I am."

Jack watched, not interfering for a moment, letting Liam have his say. Gunner didn't fight him or pull away, allowing the attack. Liam realised at that moment Gunner was taunting him, so Liam would punish him. He hated himself as much as anyone else in that room did, probably more so. Liam relaxed and let go, allowing Gunner to take a deep rasping breath.

"You're right, I'm not worthy of any of you, but I need your help."

The room went silent at his request, and the men glanced to one another in question. Jack took the lead. "Why would we help you?"

"Because you're good men."

"No, we aren't. We kill, we maim, and all in the name of our Queen."

"Yes, you are because you don't hurt innocents and you have a code."

"A code you seem to have thrown away."

Gunner hung his head before he tipped it up to Jack. "I had my reasons."

Jack paced slowly. "Oh, we know. Milla. We know all about your sister." Gunner's eyes widened in surprise, and Jack continued. "Yes, we know all about Milla. What I can't understand is why you didn't come to us?"

It was hard not to react to the betrayal in Jack's voice.

"I couldn't. They already had her, and if I'd told you they would've known. I couldn't take that risk."

"How would they have known?" Decker asked, speaking for the first time.

Gunner twisted to him. "I had to carry a chip with a mic and camera. If they thought for one second I'd signalled you, she would be dead."

Decker nodded but didn't say any more, just lifted his chin at Jack.

"What is this favour?"

"I need you to find my sister and rescue her. I thought I could do as they asked but I can't. I can't lose her either." His anguish and pain were on display for all to see, and Liam noted the dark circles under Gunner's eyes. The man was exhausted, hanging on by a fraying rope. Liam thought of the women in his life, those he thought of as sisters and wondered what he would have done. He liked to think he would've done things differently, but would he? He didn't know, and much as he hated it, his ire at Gunner faded just a fraction.

"Who are they?"

"A man who calls himself the Count. He has his headquarters at a strip club in London. Always has a team of highly trained muscle around, not Spec Ops but I'm guessing ex-military. He also has an Irish guy that just came on the scene. He seems high level, but I don't know a lot about him, just that the Count trusts him."

"Is the Count the top man?" Liam asked.

Gunner shook his head. "I don't think so. He talks about his boss but never mentions any details. He is meticulous about it. I'm not convinced he even knows who it is."

As Jack took all the information in, Liam knew Lopez would be working night and day with Will to uncover who the Count was, as well as trying to trace Bás.

"What did they ask you to do that you can't?" Alex stood straight from the wall as he asked the question.

"They wanted me to kill Reid and Callie Lundholm."

"And?"

"They want me to weaken Eidolon by taking out your partners. I'm sure you figured out I sabotaged missions."

"We did. What we couldn't figure out was why you failed. You had plenty of opportunities to do us all real harm, and you failed. Why?"

Gunner looked at Jack with a pained expression. "You were my brothers, the closest I had to family here. I didn't want to succeed and hurt anyone. I was trying so hard to walk a thin line, but they must have figured out what I was doing. They sent me a video of a man standing over Milla's bed." Gunner swallowed, and Liam knew this was painful for him. "They asked if she was a virgin."

Liam's lip curled in anger at the thought of the vulnerable woman being terrified by such a threat.

"I had to go all in after that."

"And if we do this favour, what will you do for us? Favours are for friends, family, or team members, not traitors."

Jack was being a hard ass, and Liam understood his stance and why he was forcing Gunner to work for this.

"Whatever you want. Name it, and I'll do it."

"I need you to stay undercover, go about your business and get me all the information I need to take these motherfuckers down."

"What about Milla?" Gunner looked scared but was holding his own with Jack.

"We'll make sure Milla is safe."

"You need to hurry. I can't hold off doing something and keep her safe."

Jack tipped his head to Decker, who moved forward with the laptop and hit play. They all looked on as Gunner watched the video of Fortis rescuing Milla.

He looked at Jack with hope in his eyes. "She's safe?"

"Yes."

Gunner sagged as if he was a balloon with all the air sucked from him, his head hanging as he sucked in vast pulls of air. "Thank you."

Liam could see his old teammate was sincere as the tension left his shoulders in a visible sigh. Liam was pleased they could do that for him even though he'd betrayed them. He could see now Gunner wasn't evil, misguided maybe, but he'd lost his way. If he were honest, there had been many a time when he'd been close to losing his own way.

"They won't believe I had nothing to do with this. How will I repay you?"

"Because this is the video the men who are blackmailing you will see." Decker hit play and Gunner watched, before he looked away, his face ashen.

"You'll go to them, tell them you received this through the post, and you want to see us all burn for what we did."

"They may not believe me."

"They will because you're not our only inside man."

"Oh?" Gunner angled his head to Jack in a query, but Jack shook his head.

"That's privileged information. But you'll leave any information for us in a chat room for this game." Jack showed Gunner an app that had been added to his phone by Will, Jack's tech genius brother who worked for Fortis.

"I understand. So, what now?"

"Now you get thirty minutes to visit with your sister to settle in your mind she's safe, and then you go back undercover."

Gunner nodded as Alex moved to release the restraints at his wrists and legs. Gunner stretched and offered a grateful smile. "Thank you." He looked at the four of them individually before he spoke again. "For what it's worth, my decision was the wrong one. I'll regret losing what I had with you all for the rest of my life."

Liam nodded but didn't speak. What could he say to the man that he didn't already know? They had to move forward now.

"I'll have Waggs and Alex escort you to see Milla." With that, Jack and Alex left the room, as he and Decker followed.

Liam knew there'd be much discussion on this now, but he needed a minute of fresh air first. He walked to the exit at the back and opened the door, feeling the camera follow him as he did.

His feelings towards Gunner had changed wildly during that interrogation, although to call it an interrogation was false. Gunner had given up the information readily. Taking some cleansing breaths to rid him of the emotions clogging his head, he turned to go back in and saw Jack striding down the hall towards him, a pissed off expression on his face.

"What?"

"I just had a call from Princess Taamira."

Liam groaned at her name. The woman drove him crazy with her demands and her stuck up behaviour. Yet, when he was with her, he couldn't help but wonder what she would feel like soft and pliant beneath him, if she'd only put all that fire to good use and let go of her prissy ways.

"What now?"

"She just fired her security team and is demanding you fly out to her."

"For fuck's sake." Liam hung his head as he massaged his neck.

"You need to find out what happened."

"Fine, I'll be on the first flight out. But if I wring her pretty neck, you have to post bail."

Jack chuckled. "Deal."

CHAPTER TWO

Taamira paced the length of her private suite, rubbing her hands together in agitation as she did, before spinning and returning to the open laptop on her desk. A picture of her working out in the private gym, a room only she used, was splashed across the sensationalist magazine that had been dogging her for months.

Taamira sighed as she looked at the picture. What upset her was not that the photo showed her in tight-fitting clothes that were banned in public by her religion, it was the fact the only people who had access to that room were her private security guards. She shuddered as a feeling of vulnerability invaded her body.

Taamira glanced sharply at the door of her bedroom suite, where she had closed herself from the main room as the knock came.

Her head of security's voice came through the door. "Princess, it's Derek. I'm here with the team. We need to speak with you."

Taamira took a cleansing breath as she weighed up what she should do. The only people who could have leaked that photo was her security team, but she had no idea which one of them it had been. She'd not been so vulnerable and exposed since the attack that had changed her life. Changed her entire outlook on her family, on the privileged position she was in, and how she could use it for good.

Indeed, the men of Eidolon were the only people who allowed her vulnerability to disappear and gave her confidence. Her safety when she was with them wasn't a consideration it was so natural. The men and women from Fortis gave her the same vibe. But most especially Liam, with his surly attitude, loud vulgar vernacular, and gentle eyes. He irritated her and sparred with her, not caring for her position as a Princess. No, Liam treated her as a woman, and for some reason, she knew she could be herself with him.

Taamira even enjoyed the arguments they had and often found herself doing or saying things to initiate them. As the knock came again, she found herself having to make a decision regarding her security team. She had only one choice, and as she made it, she straightened her spine and walked to the mirror. Studying herself, she made sure not a second of doubt was evident on her face, nor a hair out of place. Her royal demeanour securely in place, she strode confidently to the door and pulled it open.

Derek took a step back as she moved past him, her head high, neck long as her mother had taught her, sure she looked every inch the regal Princess of the Isle of Eyan.

"Ask your team to assemble in the lounge area immediately." Her voice was haughty and demanding, but it got her the deference she needed in this situation. She may not show it, but on the inside, she shook with nerves. There was a snake in her garden, and she needed to be careful.

"Your highness?" Derek cocked his head in question as he tried to assess her mood, but she hid even the slightest sliver of emotion from him. Derek was not a small man, but she had never sensed danger from him, and she didn't now, but she couldn't take the risk.

"Gather your team, now." Her voice was ice as she spoke, and she saw the surprise in the man's eyes as he correctly read her mood and the flinty tone as she gave her order.

Derek dipped his head and walked to the door, poking his head around it, ordering his team to do as she had bid.

Taamira resisted the urge to straighten her clothing in a show of nerves as she watched the other four men walk towards her and stand a few feet away. They varied in size, all were large, with compact muscles and a similar vibe to the Fortis men, although she didn't get that calm confidence from these men that she did with Fortis and Eidolon—something was missing.

Taamira faced the men knowing one of them had betrayed her and still had no idea who it was. All of them had been pleasant with her and seemed good at their jobs. That they would do this shouldn't shock her, and in some ways, it didn't, but it did sadden her.

"I am sure you have all seen the picture which was leaked to the press of me in the gym yesterday." She eyed each man individually, wishing she were better at reading people.

"Princess," Derek began, but she held up her hand to silence him.

"Given the fact that the only people who have access to that room are the five of you, I have no option but to terminate your employment with immediate effect."

Five shocked faces looked back at her, and the men began to speak.

"Your highness, I assure you a full investigation is underway," Derek began.

Taamira turned her gaze on the man who was in charge of this team tasked with keeping her safe from people who would do her harm. Instead, they had invaded her privacy and made her feel weak. "I am glad for that, but it does not change the fact that I can no longer trust any of you with my privacy or my safety. Therefore, you are relieved of your duties. Effective immediately."

Derek locked eyes with her, and she held her ground even as her hand began to tremble. Then he nodded, and she almost sagged with relief.

"As you wish, Princess. But I will remain in the vicinity until a replacement is appointed. To leave you without any protection is not in my nature as a guard or as a man." Derek then tipped his head and ushered his stunned men from the room.

Taamira called to him as he got to the door. "I will have your key passes."

She held out her hand to him, and he slid his hand into his pocket and handed her the pass, then took the ones his men held out. Once she had gathered them together, she nodded, and Derek and his team left the suite, closing the door silently behind them.

As he did, Taamira gripped the back of the cream leather couch and let her body sag with the weight of what she had done. Firing her entire protection was probably a very foolish move and would play right into the hands of anyone who wished her harm. But she could not be around people she didn't trust. She had lived that life, where every word uttered, or action had to be twisted inside out and examined to see if damage was the outcome they intended.

Walking on slightly wobbly legs, but with her head held high, she moved to the door and secured the chain. Then she walked to the bedroom and closed the door, pushing a chair underneath the handle.

Sitting at her desk, she looked at her image again as she moved the trackpad and woke the laptop from sleep. Her hair was wet and plastered to her neck, sweat running down her chest between her breasts. The tight workout clothes would be considered scandalous among her family and her people, and she worried what they would think. But as she looked at her reflection, she was reminded again of the oppression her sisters faced; this seemed like one more example of that.

The men of her realm were permitted to wear whatever they chose, even going shirtless on the beaches. The women had to cover themselves for fear the men would not be able to control their sexual urges and they would get the blame.

While she would not have gone this far in public given a choice, she did hope to elicit change and conversation among the people of standing who created the rules in her world. Being that they were predominantly male, she knew it was an uphill battle, but ever since her sexuality was used as a weapon against her, she had known that change was needed in her country.

Men of all religions, of all lands, needed to see that women were equals. That to use the threat of rape against a woman was a charge equal to murder in her eyes and should be tried and judged as such in every country.

For now, though, she had to figure out what she would do regarding her safety and only one person came to mind.

Liam.

Picking up her phone, she knew if she called him, he might refuse, the thought of being rejected by him scared her more than the threat. She called Jack instead, knowing he would enforce his cooperation if she demanded it.

Once again pulling her mental shield into place and putting on the mantle of a Princess, she made the call.

"Yes?" Jack was curt and to the point, but he had also offered his own life to protect his sister-in-law, and she knew for a fact she would never have survived that attack without him.

"It's Taamira." She'd asked him to drop the Princess a long time ago, even as she forced Liam to use it.

"What can I do for you, Taamira?" Jack asked in a gentle tone that she had come to expect from him. It was almost brotherly, and she wished with all her heart her own brother had been more like Jack.

"I'm in a bit of bother."

"Oh?"

She heard him stop moving and knew she had his full attention. "I fired my security team ten minutes ago."

"You what?"

Taamira heard the controlled anger in his voice. "I had too, at least one of them has betrayed me and took a picture of me in the gym. It is plastered all over the media."

"I'll have someone on a plane in the next hour."

"I want Liam."

She waited for Jack to reply to her demand. She always asked for Liam, and she knew it drove both Jack and Liam crazy that she was so demanding. But the truth was, he was the one out of them all who gave her the security that she was safe. He was the man who'd seen to her safety; had stayed beside her as she dealt with the betrayal of her family. His loud, brash, annoying presence had soothed her soul, allowing her to come to terms with what had happened.

Liam had been the person who'd held her as she cried and seen her at her most vulnerable and perversely, it was the reason she forced him to call her Princess still. She needed that distance to keep her heart safe from the man who would own it if she let him because she knew he would never feel that way about her. He tolerated her at best, was kind as part of his job, but he would never love her like she feared she could love him.

It was for that reason she was haughty and snobby around him, irritating him until they bickered. Keeping her walls up when all she wanted was to let them down.

Taamira laughed inwardly without humour, noting she must be a sadist because, despite all of those things, he was the one she wanted when things went wrong.

"He'll be on a plane in the next hour," Jack confirmed.

"Thank you, Jack."

"No problem, Princess."

Taamira hung up. Knowing Liam was on his way allowed her to breathe easier, the fear tightening her belly lessening slightly.

CHAPTER THREE

THROWING his Bergen over his shoulder, Liam moved towards the lift in the hotel in central Madrid. The concierge had been expecting him and even recognised him from previous visits, handing him a pass for the elevator that accessed the top floor of the Regent Grand. As the doors closed, Liam ignored his irritation of the fact he was back here, instead wondering at the excitement underneath.

He found he liked sparring with the Princess, who still insisted on her title when he addressed her. But even that little annoyance had him fighting the smile that played at his lips. The woman was smart as hell, funny, stubborn as shit, and so totally out of his league. That didn't stop his dick from getting hard every time she came at him with her fire and attitude though.

Using the key, he opened the door to her suite; he'd catch up with Derek in a little bit. He'd called as Liam left for the airstrip with an update, telling him a bit of what had gone down. Liam had been furious to hear that one of the men he'd personally selected for this job had betrayed Taamira, and him as well. It left him feeling guilty and responsible for her current predicament.

He stepped through and yelled, "Honey, I'm home." But before the last word left his mouth, he felt a breeze as something whistled past and turned to see a knife embedded in the wall beside his ear. Twisting quickly, he caught sight of the Princess, with her hand over her mouth in horror.

"What the fuck are you doing, woman?"

He glared at her, and her hands dropped as her feet seemed to come unglued from the plush cream carpet. Princess Taamira rushed to him and stopped a few feet away, running her eyes over his body in a way that shouldn't make him want to take her to bed, but did. He wasn't in a very forgiving mood at that moment though, so continued to glare.

"I wasn't expecting you so soon," she said as if that answered all his questions.

"So, you thought you'd throw a knife at anyone who walked through the door?" He turned and eyed the knife before returning his glare to her. "You could've frigging scalped me with that thing."

He watched as her shoulders sagged and hated his words were the reason. She had been trying to protect herself, and he should be praising her, not being an asshole about it.

"You're right, I'm sorry." Her voice was quiet and nothing like the feisty woman he knew. He needed the woman who'd fought, who'd held her head high, and he knew the way to get her to come out.

"I'm sorry, what?" Liam cupped his hand to his ear and cocked his head to her.

As he hoped it would, her head came up and he saw the timid look turn to imperial fire in her eyes. He almost groaned with desire for this woman he couldn't have as her neck lengthened in fury, her shoulders straightening like a warrior about to do battle.

"I take it back. I wish I'd had better aim now."

She spun on the heels of her expensive designer shoes and sauntered away. He chuckled to himself and admired the sway of her hips in the loose-fitting jewel green pants. One thing was for certain, nothing was ever boring around the Princess.

He walked to his usual room beside her bedroom suite and

dumped his bag on the bed before he went back into the main room and found her pouring herself a drink. Liam moved towards her and stopped, waiting for her to acknowledge him. He needed to give her that, so he did.

Taamira looked up as she took a sip before she lowered the glass. "Thank you."

Liam didn't make her say what for, he knew. The vulnerability had been evident in her big brown eyes, and he'd given her what she needed to be strong. He dipped his chin before he moved to grab a bottle of water from the fridge beside her.

"Tell me what happened."

Taamira moved to the couch and sat and he sat opposite her as was protocol, but he wanted to take her in his arms.

"I was using the gym yesterday and didn't notice anything amiss. I've done it for the last four weeks, but then this morning, I saw this image online." Taamira handed him her mobile phone, and he heard her sharp intake of breath as their fingers brushed. His eyes shot to her; she was looking down at the picture as if it might come to life.

With an effort, he dragged his eyes to the image and his breath drew in but for a different reason. It showed the Princess working out, her clothes moulded to her body, her face flushed and make-up free. She looked like a goddess come to life, but it wasn't that emotion that caused him to growl. No, it was fury that someone had done this to her, knowing how she loved her people and how they would react to this. He wanted to get his hands on the person who'd taken it and rip their bloody throat out.

Liam fought back his anger, needing to keep things professional and work out what had happened. That could only happen if he kept a clear head. "How do you know when this photograph was taken?"

Taamira stood and came to sit beside him on his couch, her leg brushing his as she did so.

"The time on the clock behind me."

Liam dragged his eyes from her full lips to where she was pointing. The time read 15:15 on the clock behind her head. "And this is significant because?"

"Because I usually use the gym in the morning, but yesterday, I had a conference call early in the morning, so I didn't get to the gym until the afternoon."

"Do you know who was on your protection duty?"

Taamira nodded. "Yes. It was Derek, Chris, and Scott."

"Leave it with me. I'll get to the bottom of this. I'll stay and be your personal guard until I arrange some backup."

"Will you attend the conference with me?"

He heard the hesitation in her voice but just the fact she'd asked showed how important it was to her. He hesitated. The situation with Gunner was unfolding rapidly and things were changing from moment to moment. "I'll need to check with Jack and make sure he can spare me and whoever else I need for an extended period of time."

"I understand, but I'm happy to pay whatever your going rate is."

Liam gritted his teeth at her mentioning money. For some reason, the thought she had to pay someone to keep her safe didn't sit well with him. In fact, he'd refused payment thus far, and he knew Jack had too. She paid the security team he'd selected for her, but anything Eidolon did was gratis at Jack's decree.

"I don't want your bloody money. It's whether I'm free to stay." He softened his voice at the hurt look she gave him. "Let me just check. I'm sure it will be fine."

"Okay."

"We need to stay close to the hotel for now, though. All right?"

He reiterated his words of earlier, needing her to understand the situation. She may have had a security member selling images, more than likely for money which was bad enough, but he couldn't erase the threats made to her back in St Kitts.

The memory of Taamira as a hostage, frightened and vulnerable, was seared into his brain. Threats that no woman, or man for that matter, should've had levelled at them. Yes, he would keep her close until he could get back up there.

Liam frowned as he realised he could be cooped up for a while.

"That's okay. I have a speech to write anyway, so I will not be gallivanting around anywhere."

He grinned as she used words that weren't part of her native tongue. Princess Taamira spoke flawless English, but it wasn't her first language. He loved listening to the lyrical way she spoke and found he did it more than he should.

"What is the speech for?"

"There is a conference on shaping the future of young women in our societies. I am to give a speech about how they deserve the same rights as men."

Liam liked that she was doing this, not that he had any say in it, but he hated the idea of her going back to wasting her intelligent and sharp mind. Sitting beside a pool or lunching with other rich people wasn't what she had been born for. In his heart he knew Princess Taamira had been born for great things.

He found himself growing more and more invested in her future, and that was a dangerous thing because Liam didn't belong in her world and she sure as hell didn't belong in his. He looked up to see her gaze on him and in it, he saw the same desire that thrummed through his blood, mixed with an innocence that had him gripping the side of the couch to resist reaching for her.

Instead, he did what he always did. He used humour and words to distance her in a way that didn't hurt her because he'd rather cut off his arm than hurt anyone, let alone a woman who'd been stabbed in the back by the family who should've protected her.

"Well then, treacle, best you get your arse into gear and do it."

Princess Taamira looked at him slightly aghast at the way he'd spoken to her before her eyes crinkled into a scowl. "Treacle? Arse?" she repeated.

Liam had to bite back the laugh that twitched at his lips. "Yeah, you know, your aris."

Taamira looked even more confused now. "My aris?"

"Yes, treacle, you know the thing you sit on."

Her look of indignation was priceless. "You mean my bottom."

"Yes, that's what I said, treacle."

He watched her eyes squint at him again at the word treacle. "And what does that mean?"

"Treacle means sweet. It's a term of endearment."

He watched her face as she thought on it for a second before she stood. "You will not refer to my bottom as an arse or an aris. Is this understood?"

Her haughty manner was back, and Liam already missed her closeness as she moved towards her room. She turned and leaned her hand on the jamb as she raised an eyebrow waiting for his response.

"Yes, Your Highness, I won't call your bottom an arse or an aris again."

"Better yet, how about we don't speak about that part of my body at all?"

"But that would be such a crying shame, treacle, because it's so worthy of discussion."

He watched as heat suffused her cheeks and warmth lit her eyes before she moved through the door and slammed it shut on him.

Liam grinned, happier than he had been in ages. He was here, and he had a lot of work to do, first finding out which arsehole had betrayed Taamira and then ensuring she was safe until she could make her speech. After that, Liam didn't know, but for now, he was happy to have provoked a blush out of her. She also hadn't demanded he didn't call her treacle, and in his book, it was a green light to do just that.

Even though he had started off the conversation wanting to put distance between them, he had, in fact, brought them closer. Yet, instead of making him unhappy, it had the opposite effect.

CHAPTER FOUR

SHE HAD MANAGED to avoid Liam since last night's encounter. Staying in her bedroom suite, having a bath, writing a few letters to her young nieces who very much enjoyed receiving them, and generally puttering around until it was time for bed.

Taamira had heard Liam moving about in the suite and for the first time in weeks had fully relaxed, safe in the knowledge that this man would protect her. More than physically, she was safe to be herself, didn't have to watch every move in case it ended up on the news.

As she applied mascara to her dark eyelashes to give her wide eyes an even more sultry appearance, she thought about last night. It had started off horribly with her nearly embedding a knife in his head and then calmed as she told him of her fears over her security. He had taken her concerns seriously, not ridiculing her or making out she was overreacting. The evening had then gone a little awry as he seemed to bait her into a reaction. Using the strange slang to describe her bottom and calling her treacle of all things.

The first had scandalized her, but it had also made her think of him thinking of her arse as he put it and that had her grinning giddily, a warmth in her belly she perhaps should not enjoy around this man. Having googled treacle and finding that it was indeed a term of endearment that meant sweetheart or sweetie, she let warm delight ripple through her all over again. She liked that he called her that as it was something she had never had before.

Now, as she added a last touch of gloss to her lips, she stood and walked to the bedroom door, noticing as she did she hadn't locked it as she had every other night.

Liam was in the living room area, his phone to his ear. As she moved past him, he turned and nodded, his eyes running over her from top to bottom, stopping for a split second on the curves of her rear end. Taamira didn't acknowledge it, but as she twisted away from his eyes, she let a smile curve her lips.

Her usual breakfast of sliced fruit and yoghurt with juice and tea were waiting for her as she moved to the dining area, Liam's deep voice a comfort as she sat to eat.

Taamira looked up as he strode into the room, looking masculine, and strong in a black t-shirt and athletic shorts.

"Morning, treacle." His smirk was sexy and so slight it was almost impossible to see unless a person had studied the man and she was embarrassed to say she had.

"Good morning, Liam. Did you sleep well?"

"Like a baby, Princess. I woke every two hours wanting food."

His words had her smiling back at him as he sat catty-corner to her and stole a strawberry from her plate, popping it into his mouth and chewing. Taamira watched him do it, wondering why she was letting him take such liberties with her. Calling her by a nickname, stealing food from her plate, all things that would never be permitted in her country. In fact, it was not something she'd ever allowed, yet when Liam did these things, far from thinking it was a breach of etiquette, it gave them an intimacy she enjoyed.

It was a silly notion really but every time he did something like that, the gap between them seemed as if it didn't exist. She was a person and so was he and she was so lonely, craving real human contact and having no way to get it. Would it be so bad to allow him these intimacies? Perhaps it would, but she needed a friend at the very least. Certainly, more than she needed him to adhere to protocol. The fact that her body and her heart wanted more than friendship from him wasn't something she could acknowledge right now.

"What are the plans for the day, Princess?" He watched her closely as he sat forward, leaning in towards her, his muscled forearms resting on the glass table.

"I have to write this speech, and so far, it is evading me." She was frustrated as she knew what she wanted to get across, but the actual content sounded pithy and boring.

"You'll get there," Liam said with complete confidence. "That was Jack on the phone. He's sending Mitch and Waggs as back-up. They should be here around three-ish."

"Oh, that is good news." Taamira patted her mouth with a napkin and took a sip of her tea.

A silence fell between them which she had the desire to fill but she had no idea what to say. Thankfully, he saved her from doing so.

"I'm going to work out on the balcony while you write. When the guys get here, I'll go and see Derek and see if we can find out what the hell went on."

Taamira watched his jaw tighten as he said the words. She stood from her seat and tucked it neatly back in before looking back at Liam who had followed suit. "I will leave you to it then." She offered him a polite smile before she turned on her heel and went to her desk in the corner of the lounge area.

Out of the corner of her eye, she watched Liam move to the balcony, leaving the door open as he knew she liked. Taamira loved the fresh air, liking the breeze on her skin. It was the little things that he remembered that gave the warmth an extra glow in her belly, a squeeze in her chest.

Opening the laptop, Taamira signed into her personal cloud storage before pulling up the speech she was trying to write for the conference. She began to read through it, hating every word and inwardly groaning at the clichés. Deleting the entire thing, she sat and looked at the blank page.

She knew what she wanted to say, what points she wanted to raise, the impact she needed this to have, but it was falling short in every direction. Taamira closed her eyes and sighed. Resting her head in her palm, she thought of the girls in her country, of her nieces, who as young teens admired her and followed her example. It annoyed her brother and sister-in-law immensely. Taamira wondered if that was why her brother had thrown her to the dogs when those men attacked her.

Even now, she still struggled with how her family had reacted, blaming her, and turning their backs. Treating her as less than human because she had the audacity to be born a woman in a male-oriented country. Even now, over eighteen months later, she refused to speak with any of them.

They had tried to contact her, but she would not hear of it. Whatever they had to say would never be enough, never excuse the treatment she had received. Perversely, it had been the way the people of Fortis and Eidolon had treated her and been so kind that had changed her outlook on life.

They had put their necks on the line for a stranger, an arrogant one at that. She had thought she could be imperious with her captors and it had cost a man his life. She still saw his face in her nightmares and would carry the guilt for eternity. However, the strangers who'd saved her hadn't abandoned her; they had rallied. It was that kindness and respect that had woken her to her own failings and selfishness.

Her ears caught the sound of a grunt, and she turned in the direction of the noise to see Liam doing biceps curls. Sweat was dripping down his face and neck, and Taamira watched mesmerised as his muscles bulged. The concentration on his face one of the sexiest things she had ever seen. That was until he stood with his back to her and stripped the wet shirt from his body, flinging it casually to the ground at his feet.

Her tongue touched her bottom lip as she turned more fully to watch, without even realising she was doing it. His back rippled as he went to the ground and began doing crunches as if they were the easiest thing in the world. She knew for a fact they weren't, having already done hers in the privacy of her room that morning and not getting anywhere near the amount he was doing.

Taamira found herself standing at the door to the balcony. She almost jumped as he flipped and began doing press-ups at an almost alarming speed. His breath was coming fast, and she could hear the effort it took him. Her mind conjured up the same sounds, but in her imagination, he worked her body with the same rigour.

A flush moved across her cheeks at the thought of what a man like Liam could do to her body. She had no experience with men, barely a kiss, and certainly no sexual contact. It was improper for a woman of her stature and title to have boyfriends. Her father had tried on more than one occasion to arrange a marriage for her, but she had refused, not wanting a man forced on her.

She may well be a fool, and God knew she had been called one by her brother many times, but she wanted love. Taamira wanted a man whose whole life centred on her, one who could be her entire world. Not a man who wanted her for her title or her family's money, or even her own money.

So that meant at her advancing age of twenty-six, she was a virgin. It was embarrassing to admit to herself, and she knew in her heart she'd never have what it took to hold a man like Liam Hayes, but oh, the daydream was sweet.

She was so engrossed in her sexy fantasy she didn't realise Liam had stopped working out and was watching her.

"Like what you see, Princess?" He was looking at her with hooded eyes.

His voice had lost the typical humour and held a gravelly, growl about it that had her thinking of whispered words and silk sheets.

Falling back on her snark to hide her humiliation at being caught ogling him like a he was a cool glass of water in the Sahara Desert, she bit out, "I have no idea what you mean."

A twinkle came to his impossibly blue eyes and his lip quirked appealingly. "Of course you do, treacle."

"I was just coming to close this door. All of this noise and grunting is distracting me."

"Apologies, Princess."

Taamira had nothing to say to that, so with one final look she went to close the door but wanting the last word she barked, "And put a damn shirt on."

Taamira spun and walked towards her desk, but as she did, she glanced back and saw Liam slipping a t-shirt over his head, a grin on his lips as he winked at her.

She scowled back at him, but it only made him smile wider. Damn that man was a menace to her equilibrium, but as she walked away, her step was lighter than it had been in weeks.

CHAPTER FIVE

LIAM WALKED to the door of the suite, peering through the peephole even though he already knew who was on the other side. Satisfied, he opened the door and admitted Mitch and Waggs. The call to warn him they were on their way up was protocol, allowing them the knowledge that if the doorbell went and no call had been received, it was treated as hostile until they knew differently.

Closing the door, Liam bit back the questions on the tip of his tongue about Gunner and the situation there when he saw Princess Taamira walk in. She was wearing loose pale peach trousers that skimmed the tips of her high heeled shoes and a cream blouse with a wide but modest neckline and sleeves ending at her elbow in some sort of ruffle. It shouldn't scream sex, but as she arched her long smooth neck to greet the other two men, Liam tried to douse a ripple of desire that shot through his dick.

What he wouldn't do to wrap that long black wavy hair around his fist and watch those full lips take his cock. It was a useless dream for so many reasons he couldn't count them all. The most apparent being she was a princess, and he was a cockney wide boy.

Another was the fact that she was a virgin and he would never take that from her, knowing he had nothing to offer her in return. Not that she would let him, they could barely be in the same room without taking a swipe at each other. As much as he enjoyed that, he knew it was not conducive to a long-term relationship.

Turning instead, he introduced his friends. "Waggs, Mitch, you remember Princess Taamira."

Waggs offered his hand which Taamira graciously took and then did the same with Mitch.

"It's good to see you both again. Thank you for coming to my aid. I appreciate this may have caused some difficulties being such short notice."

Mitch offered her a lopsided grin that had more than one woman melt into a puddle of goo before he broke out the South London charm. "It's entirely my pleasure, Princess Taamira."

Liam watched as Taamira blushed, and shot Mitch a glare, which slid off the man as if he was Teflon.

"Are you both from the same place?" Taamira asked, pointing between him and Mitch.

Liam could see how they might sound vaguely similar to someone who didn't know the London accent well, so he tried not to be offended. "Mitch is from South London and I'm from the Eastend of London."

"Oh," Taamira said, clearly not understanding the difference.

"The short answer is yes, we are, Princess," Mitch added coming to her aid again.

"Well, I am sure you have lots to do, so I will leave you to get settled in." With that, she turned on her heel and walked from the room.

Liam watched her leave, his eyes never leaving the sweet sway of her hips. He glanced back at Mitch and Waggs who were sporting wide grins. "What?" he asked sharply.

Mitch strode to him and laid a heavy hand on his shoulder as Waggs moved in beside him. "You, my friend, are so fucked."

Liam frowned. "I ain't got a Scooby Doo what you're talking about."

Mitch grinned. "If you say so, mate."

"How about you give us an update on the state of play with the Princess' security detail," Waggs asked changing the subject.

Liam led the two men out onto the balcony that wrapped around two sides of the suite. He moved far enough away that Taamira wouldn't overhear, before he turned back to them, his arms crossed over his chest. "I haven't had a chance to speak to Derek in person yet because I didn't want to leave the Princess alone. But what he's told me so far matches with what Taamira did."

Liam's jaw tightened at the reminder of how someone had invaded her privacy. "Someone took a picture of the Princess working out and posted it all over the major social media sites, but it was leaked to a trash mag first who ran it."

"Could be an employee?" Mitch said playing devil's advocate.

Liam nodded. "Perhaps, and I'll look into that, but I suspect by the angle of the photo it was someone inside the room. It was also off her regular schedule. I would expect an employee to have done it on her normal routine."

"What makes you say that?" Waggs tipped his head in question.

"Something makes me think this wasn't a spur of the moment thing, it was calculated."

Waggs nodded, accepting his gut feeling. He, as well as all the men, knew it was a massive mistake to ignore your gut.

"Any suspects?" Mitch shoved his hands in the pockets of his jeans.

"No, but I think I'll have a better idea when I've spoken to Derek's men."

"Want us to do that?"

Liam shook his head. "No, this is my mess and I need to fix it."

Mitch dipped his chin. "This isn't on you."

"Maybe, but they're my picks, so I have to take some responsibility."

Mitch and Waggs said nothing because they knew if it were them, they would be the same.

"Can you stay with the Princess while I go?"

Waggs shrugged. "That's why we're here."

"But first, coffee." Mitch turned and walked to the suite's kitchen, Waggs on his heels. They both grabbed a mug from the fully kitted cupboard before heading to the coffee pot.

Liam was about to follow when his phone rang. "Lopez, talk to me."

"Well, hello to you too, asshole."

Liam suppressed the eyeroll and waited. "Anytime today, Lopez."

"Fine," he huffed. "I've been monitoring the guestlist for the conference that Princess Taamira is attending and I just saw Abdul al Kamali is going to be there."

Liam's entire body went still, not moving a muscle. "Say that a-fucking-gain?"

"Prince Abdul al Kamali, Princess Taamira's brother, is attending the conference with his wife."

Anger surged through Liam's body. "Piece of fucking shit."

That man had sat back while men had threatened to rape his sister on live television and then slit her throat and he'd done fuck all to help her. Even worse; he'd heard her plight and knowing not only that atrocity but also the murder of innocent men and women would take place, had turned his back.

If it hadn't been for the fact that Lucy and Jace and Dane and Lauren were getting married there in a double wedding, then he, Jack, and the Fortis team wouldn't have been on hand to stop it. He shuddered at the thought of the horror that would have befallen the beautiful, stubborn woman who was right at this second, laughing with Mitch and Waggs. The sound hit him like a punch to the gut, and he wanted to spend hours listening to her laugh, seeing her smile.

"What do you need me to do?" Lopez was waiting patiently on the other end as Liam looped it over in his brain, trying to decide on a course of action and seeing only one that was safe.

"I want to know his movements. If that fucker farts, I want to know about it."

"Okay, a little more than I wanted but fine."

Lopez hung up and Liam slid his phone back into his back pocket and brushed his hands along his short hair. He was about to do battle and he knew it was going to get ugly. Some perverse part of him looked forward to sparring with the Princess though, and that made him an even bigger dick.

Mitch and Waggs looked up as he entered and immediately sensed his mood. "What?"

"Change of plans. I need you to speak with Derek. I need to talk to the Princess."

Mitch placed his almost full cup of joe on the counter, and he and Waggs moved towards the door. He was grateful they didn't ask questions, knowing he'd update them later. He waited until they had closed the suite door behind them before he turned his attention on her.

Her big brown eyes were focused on him, the warm burnished tone of her skin reminding him of the earth covered in autumn leaves. Lips that were full and rosy and begging him to kiss them. It was a fucking attractive package, but it was the unsure way her hand fluttered at her neck, and her voice shook as she spoke that had him wanting to shield her from anything that brought her a moment's fear or pain ever again.

"Liam?"

He could see the pulse pounding in her neck as she moved closer to him. He wanted to touch it with his tongue, find out if she tasted as good as she looked, but he had to remain professional.

"I had a call from Lopez. He's been monitoring the conference you're attending and noticed a late addition to the guest list."

She was closer now, and he could smell the sweet, floral scent she wore that screamed money, and it reminded him once again of the differences between them.

"Oh?"

It was neither a statement nor a question, but he answered anyway. "Your brother and his wife are attending."

He watched her spine snap straight, pain filling her eyes as she pulled back, her emotional wall coming down. It was an amazing transformation and one he hated with a passion. He liked her smiling and relaxed with his friends, not on guard and wary of every single thing she did, worrying they would judge her.

"I see." Taamira spun away from him, and he admired the graceful line of her spine.

"You need to cancel your appearance at the conference." His words were said as a statement rather than asking her and he knew he'd made a mistake as soon as the words left his mouth.

CHAPTER SIX

SHE SPUN TO FACE HIM, heat suffusing her cheeks as anger took charge of her emotions that had been teetering since he'd come in. The look on his face had forewarned her she wasn't going to like what he said.

"Absolutely not." Taamira paced back and forth as was her want when she was angry. Her brother had taken enough from her; she would not allow him to take this as well.

"Taamira."

She heard the warning in his voice but ignored it as she turned to glare at him. "Do not *Taamira* me. I am not some little woman to be cowed by a man. I am a Princess, and I will do as I please." Her head was high as she shot daggers at him, but fear was forcing her words to come out wrong. She sounded like a spoilt brat, when it was, in fact, a reaction to being told what to do by yet another man.

All her life she'd been dictated to, told what to wear, what to think, and what to say. She had thought she had got away from that, got away from having her life ruled by men who didn't care enough about her to step up when she needed them.

"You may be a Princess but you're acting like a damned spoilt child, one who has just had her toys taken away."

Taamira drew in a sharp breath and stopped her pacing to glare at him. He looked equally annoyed; his brow drawn down, hands on his hips as he returned her glare. The blue of his eyes a stormy navy that she should *not* find attractive given the situation.

"This is fucking serious, treacle. Your life is at risk. You could be hurt, you could be fucking killed. Yet you're huffing and puffing like a brat."

That snapped her out of her desire induced funk. "How dare you speak to me like that."

Her breath was coming in harsh heaves now as she stepped towards him without fear, her words coming through teeth clenched in an effort to control her ire. The dangerous vibe pulsing from him didn't make her back down. This man did not cause fear in her. Taamira knew deep in her soul he would never harm a hair on her head, and it gave her the freedom to argue in a way she never had before.

He looked down at her, his turbulent eyes on her lips, the hot air around them filling with a pulse of electricity that beat in tandem with her heart.

"I dare, Princess, because it's my stupid ass that will stand between you and a bullet. I dare because you're behaving like a naive four-year-old."

His jaw was practically granite, and she saw the five o'clock shadow and wondered if he'd shaved today or if it had just grown back from this morning. It was distracting her slightly from her tirade and train of thought. She gave herself a tiny shake to free the spell he seemed to weave over her.

"I am not."

"Are too," he retorted, and foolishly she stamped her foot in indignation and fury at the man's stubborn behaviour.

"I will go to this conference, and I will give this speech, and you will not stand in my way."

Fighting for this was essential to show the girls and women who had been suppressed and cowed that they had a voice and she would not give it up without a fight.

Liam spun away and walked to the door of the balcony and then turned, coming back towards her with a prowl. His face a cool mask she could not read; her heart beat hard against her chest as she watched him. Liam had always had a cheeky way about him, a friendliness, even when she knew she was driving him crazy, but now he looked altogether different.

"You are the most stubborn, infuriating woman I have ever had the misfortune of meeting."

The words hit her like shards of glass, piercing her skin and scoring a wound across her heart that she hadn't seen coming and hadn't earned.

It was that more than any of his other arguments that got to her. Those words that had angry tears burning the back of her eyes. Biting down on her lip she refused to show him he'd scored a direct hit and instead spun on her heel and walked to her room, running the last few feet before she slammed the door closed behind her and letting the tears fall.

She slid down the door and sat with her back to it, knees drawn up and rested her head on them as she hugged her shins. It shouldn't hurt that he'd said what he did. Liam was just her guard, he meant nothing to her, but even as she thought it, she knew it wasn't right.

Him saying he had been misfortunate to meet her hurt more than she could have imagined. Coupled with the fact that she may have to cancel her speech, she was left feeling defeated in a way she had not felt since her attack.

Just hearing her brother's name hurt. Even now, coming to terms with the low regard he held for her caused almost unbearable pain. They had been close when she was a child, playing together in the palace gardens and hiding from the nanny when it was time for lessons. It was as they grew older his role in her life changed from playmate to domineering older brother, then they had grown apart.

Now he was going to stop her from doing her speech, and she wanted to fight for her rights, but Liam's words came back to her.

"I dare, Princess, because it's my stupid ass that will stand between you and a bullet."

That fact that he was willing to do that for her, to stand in harm's way meant she had to respect him and protect him over her own needs. She also needed to apologise and perhaps try and explain the reason she had reacted the way she had.

It was by no means necessary, but she hated the thought of a man she had come to care for thinking she was a brat. His words stung way more than they should, but she had to admit he was right; she had indeed acted as he had said, like a brat.

It didn't mean that she would forgive him for the hurt he'd caused her. His words had been said to maim, and they had hit their mark. She would apologise for her part in this, but she would not let him off the hook for hurting her, and she would guard her feelings harder than ever before.

She sat up straighter at a knock on the door behind her, swiping at the wetness on her cheeks.

"Princess," Liam called, his voice muffled by the thick door.

"Go away." Taamira was proud that her voice sounded strong.

"Open the door, treacle."

Taamira could tell from his voice that he was directly outside. She did not answer him, hoping he would leave so she could lick her wounds in peace.

"Please."

She wanted to, but she would not let him see her this way, so exposed and raw. He had hurt her once today, she would not give him the chance to do it a second time.

A vibration thudded behind her back and she guessed he must have sat, too. The image of them either side of the door popped into her head, giving them a closeness yet still keeping that barrier of safety.

"I had a best friend," he began, and she listened intently to his words, her body angled into the door, her palm touching the cool wood.

"His name was Ambrose. Best damn friend anyone could ever ask for. We went through school together, through basic training, and eventually, I followed him into the SAS. He said I was like an annoying younger brother. We were only a few months apart in age, but I guess I always looked up to him."

Liam stopped, and Taamira held her breath, waiting for more, and he didn't disappoint.

"When he left the military and joined Eidolon, I followed again. We were more than friends, we were brothers. He would've died for me, and I would have done the same for him. He met a girl, her name was Gail and they had a son Natai."

Taamira could hear the smile of affection his voice when he said that name.

"Kid was the spitting image of his dad, and I was so honoured when they asked me to be his godfather. Then one day we got a job."

Taamira could practically touch the pain and remorse flowing through the door it was so strong.

"Ambrose was on guard duty for a child and his mother, the people after her were sick pieces of work and we were their protection. I was twenty or so minutes late, and when I got there, Ambrose was on the ground with paramedics working on him."

Taamira pulled in a shaky breath as she stroked her fingers along the wood, wishing it were Liam.

"They were attacked, and the kid's mum taken. Ambrose was shot in the shoulder, nothing too serious, but as he went down, he hit his head on the stone steps. They did everything they could, pumped him with drugs and did untold procedures, but he never woke up, and four days later, my best friend took his last breath on this earth."

A fresh tear slid down her cheek, but this time it wasn't for her plight; it was for Liam and the grief she knew he still carried and probably always would.

"I lost my best friend, his girl, and my godson that day. Gail never forgave me for not being there, and honestly, I deserve it. But I can't lose anyone else, treacle. I don't think I have it in me to bury another person I give a shit about."

Taamira stood and slowly opened the door. She looked down and saw Liam looking up at her. His face was awash with painful memories, and she realised at that moment that what separated them as people was not a title, or privilege, but experiences. He had been through his and was still fighting, yet she was allowing what happened to her and with her family to become the hill she would die on.

CHAPTER SEVEN

LIAM LOOKED up into the beautiful brown eyes of the woman he'd hurt with his nasty words, rimmed with black mascara that had run from the tears he'd made her cry. Pain hit him in the chest, and he rubbed at the spot wondering how he had sunk even lower than he had before. Watched as his words hit their mark, her face falling even as she tried her damndest to hold her composure together. He had let her run, even as he wanted to snatch back his words.

His fear and inadequacies had him lashing out with words that caused her harm, cutting her deep. Yet here she was, bending and going to her knee before she sat beside him. He knew fear was only part of the reason he'd lashed out. The other part was his attraction to her and the fact he couldn't do a fucking thing about it.

Her position alone put them leagues apart, add in her spirit and her sweetness that she hid from almost everyone under a veil of tartness and haughtiness, and he knew she was too good for him.

"I'm sorry about your friend."

The simple words meant more than they should, and Liam's chest clenched in familiar pain at the reminder he'd never see his friend again. "Me, too."

"He sounds like a great man. Will you tell me more about him sometime?"

Her question held genuine interest. It was a skill that seemed effortless from her, and she made people think they were her entire focus, that she cared about what they said be they a porter or a prince, she gave them all equal measure.

"Yes. One day I'll tell you all about Ambrose. Would you like to see a picture of Natai?" He found himself asking her a question he'd never intended, opening up a level of sharing that went beyond that of guard and principle.

She nodded, and a smile came to her lips; lips he could hardly tear his eyes away from. "Yes, please."

Liam leaned on one hip as he took his wallet from his back pocket and flipped it open before showing her the picture of Natai that Gail had sent him. It was the only contact he'd had with her since Ambrose was buried. Natai was looking at the camera, his wide grin infectious, eyes bright with mischief, on his first day at school.

Taamira took the image from him and looked at it with warmth in her eyes. "Oh, he is precious. Look at that smile, it could melt an iceberg."

"Yeah, he lights up a room with his smile, always seemed to command a room even as a young child." Liam spoke with pride he hadn't earned for the boy he loved as if he was his own.

"You love him very much."

Taamira said the words as a statement, not a question and Liam didn't try to hide it.

"I do, yeah."

"Do you get to see him often?"

Liam's grin faltered at the question, and he shook his head. "No, since Ambrose it's been tricky. Gail blames me, and she's right," he added quickly, not wanting Taamira to think wrong of the woman his friend had loved.

"She was hurting, but it is no excuse. I am coming to see that whatever pain we have does not trump the pain of another, and it is wrong to believe what we feel is more important."

Liam stayed quiet, not knowing what to say to that. Was Gail's pain worse than his own? Perhaps it was but then again, maybe not. They had all lost a great man, and he would turn in his grave to know they hadn't stayed in each other's lives, had not clung together but instead had allowed grief to rip them apart. Maybe when this was all over, it was time to clear the air and see if they could find a way forward.

They sat in silence for a few moments as Liam tried to find the words to explain his behaviour. He reached out and twined his fingers with hers. "I'm sorry I hurt you, treacle. It was uncalled for and callous, and I am profoundly sorry."

Taamira nodded, not quite letting him off the hook but not pulling her hand away as he laid her palm against his much bigger, much rougher one.

He felt like an even bigger tool as he looked at their entwined hands, hers so soft and tiny in his. "I can't excuse the way I acted, but it was fear. If something happened to you, it would hurt," he finished lamely.

"Can I explain why I acted the way I did?" Taamira asked.

Liam tipped his head to her to go on.

"My brother was my hero. We would play hide and seek in the gardens, hide from our tutors, and sneak biscuits from the kitchen. Then one day, it all changed. He became my senior, he looked at me as not a little sister but as a woman to be cowed and ignored. He was never cruel or hurtful intentionally, but he became a man's man. The men of my country do not value the women. They do not rape or hurt them physically, but neither do they value them for anything other than becoming mothers or keeping homes."

She turned more fully to him, and he saw the light in her eyes as she spoke. "Do you know that less than five per cent of the women in my country have gone to university?"

"But you did," Liam said, knowing she had indeed studied at Oxford.

"I did, but only because my mother fought for it with every breath. I don't want my daughters or nieces to have to fight so hard for equality. I want them to be doctors and lawyers, to change the world however they see fit because they are bright, ambitious, driven. If they want to become wives and raise families, I support that too. I want them to have the choice and only by standing up and saying I am not afraid and helping them see that they matter, showing them an example to follow, can I do my small part."

The passion in her eyes was like a fire raging, its heat growing in intensity with every word she spoke. Liam found himself hanging on her every word, entranced by her spirt and determination to show those women a better way of life if they wanted it.

"I see now that you weren't a brat at all. I mistook your passion for childishness and for that, I'm sorry. If you wish to speak at the conference, then I fully support it and will be by your side the entire time, ensuring your safety." Liam knew he had settled on the right decision when the joy moved over her features.

"Truly?" she asked as if she was a child given an hour alone in a toy shop.

He grinned and dipped his head. "Truly."

"Oh, thank you." Taamira squeezed his hand and shrugged her shoulders in excitement.

"My pleasure, Princess."

He watched a frown mar her face then.

"What did I say?" he asked concerned.

She looked at him, shaking her head, the thick silk of her hair falling over her shoulder. "May I ask you a question?"

"Sure."

"When you call me Princess, is it mockingly or is it with respect that you use it?"

Liam grinned then. "I say it with affection and respect."

Her face brightened at his words. "And treacle?"

"That is with complete affection."

"I like it when you call me treacle, but I also like it when you call me Princess as you do."

"Maybe we can graduate to Taamira soon then," he said, knocking her shoulder gently with his own.

"I'm not sure about that. Do you have a nickname I can call you now that we are somewhat friends?"

"My friends call me Liam or Pyro."

"Pyro? But why?"

"I'm an explosive expert, Princess."

"Ah, then Liam it is as I don't like that other name." She wrinkled her nose in a cute grimace, and it took everything in him not to lean in and kiss her.

"I like the sound of my name on your lips, Princess." His voice had gone deep as he looked at her and thought of all the ways he wanted her saying his name, on her knees as she looked up at him, in the morning as he woke her with his mouth, in the dark of night as they shared a secret.

The mood seemed to shift, the hair on his nape lifting. There was so much sexual tension in the room, it practically buzzed. This woman had no idea what she did to him, no idea of the power she held or the sexuality she exuded, and that was why she was ten times more potent and a hundred times more off the table.

Liam leaned into her as if pulled by a force so much more powerful than he. She did the same, and it was as if an invisible line was pulling them together. Her breath feathered his face, he could almost taste the sweetness of her lips. Then a door slammed, and he heard Mitch and Waggs move inside the apartment.

"Saved by the bell," he rasped before he stood and held out his hand to her.

The flush on her cheeks was the only indication that she'd felt the same as he did, and that made the bullet they'd just dodged so much more deadly.

CHAPTER EIGHT

It was two nights later when Taamira suggested they eat at the hotel restaurant instead of being confined to the suite. There was an excellent seafood establishment with one of the top chefs in the country at the Regent Grand. Liam had discussed it with Mitch and Waggs, and they'd all agreed it was probably safe to grant her request.

The mood between Liam and Taamira was one of ease since their fight the other night, she respected his judgement, and he was careful to understand her needs. The undercurrent of sexual tension, however, was causing his balls to go blue and the number of cold showers he was taking had increased to two a day.

The one thing troubling him though was his discussion with Derek. The man had been upfront and hugely apologetic about the breach in security under his command. Liam was usually a good judge of character, and regret was oozing from the man. He'd personally spoken to the others, and he'd managed to narrow it down to two men who were tweaking his senses.

He was going to ask Mitch and Waggs to speak to them and get their opinions, and then he'd decide on what action he'd take. Liam watched as the door opened to Taamira's bedroom and she stepped out.

The woman was a fucking vision in a shimmery, cream coloured kaftan with olive green embroidery along the edge of the square neckline. He'd never thought a big swampy kaftan that hid all the beautiful curves on a woman would be sexy, but on her, it was. Fuck, who was he kidding, she could make a bin liner look hot as hell.

Her eyes met his, and she must have seen the appreciation in them because she dipped her head as a blush crept over her cheeks. Liam couldn't hide the grin which spread across his face nor the desire that her innocence evoked in him. Taamira seemed to have no clue how breathtaking she was and that was so damn attractive.

He ambled towards her feeling like a poor relation even in a crisp white shirt, navy trousers, and a navy suit jacket. Her gaze rose to his, and he let her peruse him, loving the way her coral lips parted as she did.

"Are you ready to go, Princess?" Liam held out his arm for her to proceed him.

Taamira nodded and walked towards the door of the suite, where Mitch and Waggs were already waiting on the other side. Not one to take chances, they'd already checked out the restaurant and ground floor, and nothing seemed amiss.

With ear comms in place and a mic at his wrist, he let them know they were coming. "Venus is on the move."

"Copy," Mitch replied.

As Liam reached the door, he paused before he opened it. "You look stunning tonight, treacle."

A smile of pure feminine pleasure moved across her face at his compliment. "You look very handsome too, Liam."

Liam shot her a wink and then opened the door to find Mitch. Waggs was already at the elevator with the doors open waiting. They moved as a seamless unit, each taking up a position to protect the Princess but giving her enough space to breathe. Liam would prefer to be closer, perhaps too close but as they neared the ground floor where the restaurant was situated, he became antsy, wanting to turn around and take her back to the room, wrap her up until all threats had ceased. Except that would never be the case for a woman like Taamira. With her social status and the fact she was making waves amongst some in her society, there would likely always be something.

As the doors to the elevator opened, they moved towards the lobby, Liam scanned the area as he kept his hand on Taamira to guide her. Finding nothing of interest, they moved as one towards the restaurant entrance.

They were met by the hostess who offered a flirty smile to the three men only to be met by stern faces of professionalism. Dipping her head, she quickly led them to a table in the corner of the room. As requested, there were two tables on either side kept open to give the Princess space and privacy. It also allowed her guards to have easier access to her if an incident arose.

Taamira sat, and Liam pushed her chair in closer and stepped back. She looked up at him with a tilt of her perfect neck. "Will you join me?"

He was loath to turn her down. Something in her voice and the hesitation in which she asked showed her softer side and the vulnerability she hid from the rest of the world, but he was working, and his job was to keep her safe. She saw the pause and shook her head, embarrassment creeping up her skin in a pink tinge.

She waved him off. "It's fine, don't worry."

Liam looked to Mitch for help, and his friend nodded letting him know they had this, and Liam blew out a breath, the pain in his chest easing as he sat and grinned at her. "And pass up the chance to share dinner with a beautiful woman? Not gonna happen, sweetheart."

Her smile told him it was the correct decision.

"Can I get you anything to drink, Your Highness?" the hostess asked, now oozing professionalism as Taamira placed her napkin on her lap.

"Do you have any alcohol-free sweet cider?"

"We have an apple and pear cider that is lovely."

Taamira nodded. "Perfect, thank you."

The woman looked at Liam. "And for you, sir?"

"Just water, please."

"Your waiter will be Miguel, here are your menus." The woman laid them on the table in front of them and left.

Liam looked around, satisfied that Mitch and Waggs were covering their backs.

He glanced at Taamira. "Cider, treacle?"

She glanced up from her menu, her eyelids blinking slowly before she gave him a small tilt of her lips. "I tried it in London when I went to the wedding of Prince Luke and Princess Caroline. It's extremely sweet and fruity and tastes like sunshine."

He wanted to reach across the table and kiss as she wrinkled her nose in an adorable way.

Luckily, the waiter came back with their drinks. "Are you ready to order?"

Liam lifted his menu and glanced at it quickly, it was a seafood restaurant, but he had never taken to seafood really unless it was wrapped in batter and served with chips smothered in salt and malt vinegar. "Princess?" he asked.

"I would like the turbot with peppercorn sauce, please."

Miguel nodded and tilted his head to Liam. "And for you, sir?"

"Ribeye steak, rare, with chips and beef dripping, please."

The waiter left, and Liam found the silence a little disturbing. It was a little like a date, but one where he had his friends watching him, and one where he shouldn't be lusting after the woman opposite.

"I've made things awkward, haven't I?" Taamira stated.

He glanced at her and saw the sadness in her eyes. "No, it's not that. I like being with you, Princess, and that's the problem. I could spend all day talking to you, watching you work or even watching you read a book, and that isn't how it should be. Apart from the fact you're so far out of my league you're practically on a different planet, I'm your personal protection, and the truth is, I want this to be way more personal than is sensible."

"I am not out of your league, Liam. You are out of mine."

Her words shocked him. "What in the hell?"

"It's true, you have experienced life in ways I can never imagine, both good and bad I am sure. You have made love to a woman, had love from a woman. Defied the odds against enemy combatants that I could not envisage. It is you who is out of my league, not the other way around."

Liam looked at her, dumbfounded by her words, both because she thought that and now because he couldn't get the image of making love to her out of his head. He moved in his seat to make room for the growing bulge in his trousers. Thankfully, the waiter picked that moment to deliver their food, sparing him a few moments to think.

With the food in front of them, he watched her lift her fork and place a delicate piece of turbot into her mouth. He watched her chew and found the way she closed her eyes to enjoy her food as erotic as some women on a stripper's pole.

"Fuck," he growled.

Her eyes popped open at his expletive.

"Princess, you're gonna be the death of me."

"Why?"

"You make me crazy. I want to kiss you all the time, I want to bury myself inside you so bad I can hardly think straight, and now you think I'm out of your league. You're everything I'm not. I'm not a hero, and I'm definitely not a prince. I'm a boy from the Eastend, a scrapper. I should be shot for even thinking the things I do about you. You should be running for the hills."

"You make me feel safe." Her words were simple but said quietly and with emotion in her voice. "You make me feel seen and as if I am not alone in this world."

Liam shook his head. "You're not alone."

"I am. My family is all but lost to me. I have no real friends, and the ones I do have would stab me in the back at the chance to be in favour with my father."

Liam's chest constricted at her words, and he recognised the loneliness she hid so well from others. With her grace and kindness, she never let it show that her world was less than perfect.

"You have me, treacle. I'm your friend, and you have Mitch, Waggs, and Jack."

"You are my personal protection, Liam, not my friend. And before you react, those are your words, not mine."

She was right; he had said that, but it was becoming more evident by the second that he wanted more, and she needed more. Could he be friends with this woman without it falling into something more? The truth was he didn't know, but he wanted to try, for her sake and his own. It may not be the smartest idea he'd ever had, but he was jumping anyway.

"I want to be your friend if you'll have me?"

He watched the look of happiness spread over her face as she nodded. "I would like that very much."

"Well, then let's eat, friend."

They ate and chatted and the more they did, the more he realised he'd been a fool because Taamira was intelligent, she was funny, and she was gracious. Every little thing she did seemed to make his dick twitch and that was very unfriend-like.

It was hard to regret it though because as they finished their meal with coffee and delicate little cakes that were barely bite sized, he realised he couldn't remember a time when he'd enjoyed himself more. He would have to be careful not to let his growing affection for this woman show or cloud his judgement in any way.

"Ready to head up?"

"Yes, thank you, Liam. This is the best non-date date I have ever been on."

Liam winked and smiled. "Me too, Princess."

He pulled out her chair and turned to Mitch and Waggs, back in protection mode once more, not that he'd ever really left it. He still knew exactly who had entered the room and where they were seated, despite the fact he'd been having dinner with such a beautiful and engaging woman. It was just a part of who he was now.

As they left the restaurant and walked across the crowded lobby, he moved closer to Taamira. It was difficult to see all the potential threats as a large group were checking in and being very loud.

Just as they stepped up to the elevator, a man ran from the crowd towards them, a gun waving in his hand as he shouted, "Traitor."

Liam was over Taamira in a second, flattening her to the ground, his body shielding her as he saw Mitch and Waggs tackle the man, taking him to the ground a few feet from where they now lay.

"Whore. You are a traitor to your country," the man spat at Taamira as Liam lifted her from the ground, his body between her and the man.

Mitch shook him. "Shut your fucking mouth before I do it for you."

The man glared at Mitch but did as he was told, seeming to sense it wasn't a threat but a promise.

"Get him out of here and secured."

Waggs nodded at Taamira. "You good?"

"Yes," Liam grunted and ushered Taamira into the elevator.

He was silent as Taamira tucked in closer to his body, hers pressed down his side as he held his arm around her shoulder. Her body quaked as adrenalin left her and shock and fear took over.

Anger roared through him, and he had the urge to hit something hard, and once he had the Princess secure and knew she was okay, he knew just who it would be.

Liam got Taamira to the suite and after checking the room was clear, he led her to the bar where he poured her some water, wishing he could give her something more substantial but knowing she didn't drink alcohol.

She took the glass with a tremor in her hand, and he cupped it with his as she drank the cool liquid.

"That man wanted to hurt me."

He took the glass from her and looked into her huge brown eyes that were filled with fear and lost his distance. With one hand, he pulled her into his arms, holding her close, stroking her back as she buried her head in his neck, holding on tight to the back of his shirt.

"I won't let anyone hurt you, treacle." It was a vow he would keep.

CHAPTER NINE

When Liam had put in the call to Jack earlier, he'd been surprised that his boss had been so willing to send his second in command to support them. They were fighting their own personal war on home soil against an unknown enemy, but Jack had a soft spot for the Princess. Now Alex was here and watching Taamira in the suite where she was resting after taking a sleeping pill.

He'd been proud of the way she'd pulled herself together so quickly, but also thankful. His fury at the attempt on her life was simmering, growing worse with every shiver that ran through her as his arms tightened around her. Her control and calm had soothed the beast that was roaring to be released to do serious damage to the attacker.

Liam had stayed with her until Alex got there to watch her, then he'd driven to this tiny house on the outskirts of the city, away from any form of civility. He knew the people on the streets weren't the type to call the police if they heard a scream. For his current purpose that suited him just perfectly.

Unlatching the back door, he found Mitch waiting for him, a gun resting in his hand at his side. Relaxed but ready should anyone they hadn't been expecting arrive. Liam lifted his chin in greeting, and Mitch lifted his head to indicate Liam should follow him. Twisting, he secured the lock and headed down the steps to the cellar in the tatty building.

Mitch threw him a balaclava which he donned as Mitch donned his own. While the man may realise the men questioning him were the same ones who had guarded the Princess, the uncertainty would add to the fear.

His jaw tightened, and anger flexed inside him at the sight of the man who had tried to attack the Princess—*his* Princess. He remained silent as he watched the man who was tied to the wooden chair with rope track his almost silent movements with his ears. His eyes were covered, his mouth gagged. The lack of senses was a common interrogation tactic and leaving him in silence and alone to wait was clearly getting to this man if the sweat running down his face was any indication.

Mitch had snapped a picture and sent it to Lopez, who was running his face through recognition software, seeing if they got any hits. Until they did, Liam would use his own techniques to get information taught to him by the best of the best.

Waggs was leaning on the opposite side of the room, the camera they'd been monitoring the man with catching every twitch he made. Stepping closer, he could smell the man's stale sweat, see the grease in his dark hair. Liam leaned in slowly towards the man's ear, and the stranger tensed, his back snapping straighter as he recognised someone was there, but he had no clue how close Liam was.

"What is your name?" he bellowed and almost smiled at the way the man jumped.

The man remained silent, and Liam quirked a brow at Waggs, who grinned. Liam walked behind the man and watched as he turned his head to try and track the threat his hindbrain recognised.

"Who do you work for?" Liam pulled the fabric bag from the man's head and removed his gag as Waggs directed the light directly into his eyes.

He blinked widely, the pockmarks on his face partially covered by the dark hair of his beard. The man had a similar skin tone to Taamira, and Liam had his suspicions on who this man worked for but had been taught not to jump to conclusions.

Liam brought the large K-Bar from the sheath at his back and toyed with it as he circled the man. "Don't make me ask again, motherfucker?" Liam growled.

"Long live the King."

The words had barely left the man's lips before Liam had the chair tipped on its back with the man still sitting in it, the blade of his knife pressed to his throat.

"Fucking name."

"Hassan," the man almost squeaked.

Liam paused for effect and then stepped back, righting the chair as he did. "See, wasn't that so much easier?"

The man nodded as his gaze stayed firmly on Liam, as the main threat in the room.

"Now, who do you work for?"

The man remained tight-lipped at this question, his mutinous face closing down. What Liam wanted to know was if it was fear or loyalty that kept him silent. Luckily, he knew just how to test that.

He turned and nodded at Waggs. "Find his family and have them tortured until he gives us a name." The man paled but remain silent. A loyal man would give up his loyalties to protect those he loved. "Until then, Hassan can remain here and enjoy the accommodations."

Liam heard Waggs leave and then smiled. "Now we can get started on some real torture techniques."

Hassan blanched, the colour seeping from his face as Liam pulled on black leather gloves. He didn't enjoy interrogations, but they were necessary in their line of work. Growing up on the streets of the Eastend of London while his mother worked three jobs to pay the rent, meant Liam had gotten into more than a few scrapes.

His skillset had been refined in the SAS but underneath, the kid who fought dirty still survived, and he had every intention of using whatever he had to in order to keep Taamira safe.

He landed the first blow to the man's gut, doubling him over as his breath left his body, the uppercut to his chin knocked the chair clean over. Blood exploded from Hassan's face, and he began to shriek in pain.

Liam pulled back and lifted the chair upright again. "Who. Do. You. Work. For?"

"I work for no one."

Liam shook his head. "Are you really going to do this, Hassan? Take a beating and then watch as we torture your family?"

The man was mute as blood poured down his face. Liam had barely gotten started, but this man would not last the distance and Liam had no interest in playing this game with him.

Waggs stepped back into the room and moved to Liam, whispering to him which had Hassan tensing.

"Hassan Bahri, forty-six years old, with six children no less, and a loving wife."

"Stay away from my family." Hassan bit out the words with hostility, but he lacked conviction and Liam knew it.

"My pleasure, Hassan. I have no interest in hurting anyone. All you have to do is tell me who you work for because, and make no mistake, while I don't want to hurt innocents, I will do what it takes to protect the Princess."

Hassan reared back and spat on the floor at Liam's feet. "She is a whore who flaunts the rules of her God and her King."

Liam almost rolled his eyes at the trite response. "I ain't doing this, Hassan. Names now or we pay your family a visit they won't forget."

When Hassan said nothing, Liam turned to leave and nodded at Waggs. "Let's go."

They did indeed have the address for the man's family, but it was in Eyan and while he could go, he wouldn't. The threat should be enough, and even if it wasn't, he now knew where the danger was coming from, and he could lock it down without Hassan.

"What are you thinking?" Mitch asked as they stepped into the living room they'd set up with cameras as a command base of sorts.

"It's obvious to me that the attack originates from the palace." Liam crossed his arms as he watched the man on the screen snivelling.

"You don't think he did this alone? Just some fanatic that didn't like the Princess' take on modern society being part of Eyan culture?" Waggs enquired.

"Nah, he's a pussy, and most of the Eyan people are poor. There's no way he would spend his money to come here and do this without someone funding him in some way."

Mitch tipped his head to the side. "You think it's the brother?"

"My guess is yes but we can't know for sure. I want the Princess somewhere safer."

"Home?"

"Home," Liam confirmed.

He knew having her at his home would test his resolve regarding his attraction to her, but he would not endanger her life because he couldn't control his dick. It was time to take the Princess back to Hereford.

"Let's get him locked up until we can be sure who's behind this. You two can stay with him while Alex and I get the Princess secured."

"Oh, great, we get the fugly one and you get the beauty. That seems fair."

"Can't help it. She likes me better," Liam said and laughed.

"Hmm," Waggs hummed.

Liam's jaw flexed as the unsaid words in that one sound echoed around the room. "What the fuck does 'Hmm' mean?"

"Nothing. Just be careful. A woman like that can twist you until you don't know which way is up. I'm sure she wouldn't mean to, but you guys are miles apart."

Liam resented Waggs shoving that fact down his throat when he already knew it well enough. "Know that, brother, but would appreciate it if you kept your fucking nose out of it."

Waggs held up his hands in supplication. "Meant no harm."

"Good. Now, can we just get on with our fucking jobs and stop being fannies?"

Liam didn't wait for an answer, he was angry but not just at Waggs for what he'd said but because he was right, and Liam hated it. He was falling for a woman he could never have and that sucked donkey balls.

CHAPTER TEN

TAAMIRA WAS foggy-headed from the sleeping pill she'd taken last night as they boarded the flight to the UK. Now, after some food and water, her head was a little clearer. They were speeding towards Hereford from the tiny airport where they had landed, and she had to admit she was more than a little intrigued to see the city where Liam lived.

Never getting further north than London when she'd been to the United Kingdom, she grew more enchanted with the countryside she could see as they sped past fields and fields filled with grain or cattle and horses.

Liam had explained he wanted her where he could protect her better. Away from public places as much as possible. After the fright of the man trying to attack her last night, she had readily complied. After all, she could write her speech and conduct calls for her charities and such from anywhere.

He'd told her almost nothing about where she would be staying, just that she would be safe, comfortable, and have access to space.

"Is it true there is a Cathedral here that dates back to the seventh century?" Taamira asked as Liam drove them towards the town that was his home. Alex had graciously let her sit upfront, which was a change for her. She was used to being chauffeured but found she enjoyed riding in the front.

Liam glanced at her with a frown. "I have no idea."

"But you have been to see it, right?"

"Yes, I've been to services there."

Taamira saw a slight frown mar his forehead and wondered what had caused it.

Alex leaned forward, poking his head between the seats. "The Cathedral has a stained glass window dedicated to SAS soldiers and the Special Air Service 22 regiment."

"Oh." Taamira looked at her hands in her lap; she knew she had somehow touched a nerve with Liam. "I am sorry if I upset you."

Liam's gaze swung to her, and he shook his head. "You didn't upset me. It just made me realise how long it is since I went."

"Would you take me to see it?"

Liam dipped his chin. "Yes, if I can."

Taamira smiled and then looked out of the window as they drew up outside an old brick house down a long lane. She looked up and saw it was actually a converted barn with some, if not all, of the original features. The door beside her opened, and she startled as Liam poked his head in, she'd been so lost in her admiration of this property.

"This is a truly magnificent home. Are you sure the owners won't mind us using it?"

Liam smirked and shook his head. "No, Princess, they won't mind at all."

Liam turned to Alex. "If you take the car back to work, I can use the one in the garage."

"Sure thing. Give us a call later, and we can make a plan." Liam nodded and then turned back to her. "Ready to go in?"

Taamira waved at Alex as he drove away and nodded at Liam.

Just then she heard the strangest noise. Her head whipped in the direction of the braying sound and she saw a grey donkey pop his head over a fenced-off field that bordered the drive.

"Hello, gorgeous. What is your name?" Taamira moved closer, her hand stretched out to rub his big floppy ears.

"This is Digby," Liam answered, scratching the animal under the chin.

Taamira couldn't fight the smile, her heart light with joy at the interaction with this adorable beast. "Well, aren't you just perfect."

Liam laughed. "Digby is a rescue of sorts. Aren't you, boy?"

Taamira looked sideways at Liam and saw the affection for the animal on his face. It was a side of him she hadn't expected, and she wondered how many layers this man had that nobody or at least very few got to see.

"How do you know so much about him?"

"Because Digby is mine. He'd been abandoned by the previous owners when I bought this place. It used to be a livery yard, and when the company went into administration, they walked away and left Digby to fend for himself."

Taamira looked at the vast fields surrounding the property with wonder anew, knowing they belonged to the man in front of her. "So, this is your home?"

He nodded and reached out to take her hand in his. "Come on, let's go in and I can give you the tour."

Taamira loved how small her hand was in his much larger, rougher one and the ease with which he had taken it. It was a natural reaction as if they held hands all the time, and she couldn't help the pang in her chest that this was not her reality.

Instead, she allowed him to lead her inside. The inside was as beautiful as the outside with wooden beams, open spaces, and real oak floors. At the back of the large entryway, a floor to ceiling window gave a view over the meadows at the rear of the property. Her favourite by far though was the sunroom that led out onto a large patio area surrounded by grass. It lacked flowers, but it did allow Digby to lean his head over and join them.

"He gets lonely. I should really get him a girlfriend," Liam said by way of an explanation for why the donkey lived so close to the house.

"It's beautiful, Liam. Truly, this is a beautiful home. How long have you lived here?"

"About four years." He led her back inside and filled the kettle with water as she took a seat at the large kitchen table. "I did most of the restoration work myself."

Taamira could see the pride in his face as he picked up a book and pushed it across the table to her.

Opening it, she saw a picture of what the house had looked like before the renovation. As she turned the pages, she could see the transformation take place before her eyes. She stopped at a photo close to the beginning of the project from the look of the site and looked closer.

A man had his arm around a grinning Liam who held a pickaxe in his hand. Both men were grinning widely at Digby to the side of them who seemed to be photobombing the picture. The man she assumed was Ambrose was good looking with black skin, broad shoulders, and eyes that seemed to smile as much as his lips did. The affection between the two men was evident, and she could see just from the image how a loss like that would leave a deep wound.

"He thought I was crazy buying this place at first but when he realised that the field out back was a direct walk to his house, and Natai would be able to use all this land, he was all for it."

"Did he work with you on any of it?" Her voice was soft as he came to sit beside her, placing a cup with tea in it in front of her.

He turned the book to him before he answered and eyed the photo. "Not really, he was killed a week after this photo was taken."

"I am so sorry, Liam."

"Me too. Ambrose would've loved this place. He saw the plans though, and I didn't make a single change. I wanted it to be what he saw, you know. Ambrose was my brother more than my friend, as much as I love the guys at Eidolon, it's different. Ambrose knew me back when I was nothing but a trappy asshole with holes in my shoes. We helped each other out of so many scrapes, I can't even remember half of them."

"That history is hard to replace," she said sadly.

"You had that?" he asked carefully.

Taamira nodded. "I did with Abdul before life changed and he moved on to become the heir apparent to my father."

She saw the regret cross his features and didn't want that mood to take hold of either of them.

"Do you cook?" she asked, standing from the table, and moving to the cupboards.

Liam leaned back in his chair and watched her intently as she walked around his space. "I have four dishes I cook to perfection, and everything else is a bust."

"What are they?"

"Beef curry, spaghetti Bolognese, full English, and beans on toast." He counted the meals off on his fingers as he spoke.

Taamira moved closer and looked down at him as his gaze travelled slowly up her body. A shiver ran through her, and her nipples pebbled with the desperate need for his touch, at the sudden heat in his gaze.

"Beans on toast," she said instead trying to distract herself and fighting the sudden urge to move closer and slide her ass onto his lap.

"British staple, canned beans in tomato sauce on toast." His voice was gravelly, and she liked the fact he didn't try to hide his desire.

"Doesn't that make the toast wet?"

"So moist," he said with a smirk, and she had the feeling he was not talking about toast anymore.

Taamira wanted to squeeze her thighs together to ease the sudden bolt of desire there. He moved to stand quickly, and she took a step back, but he wrapped his arm around her waist and pulled her closer to his front. Her breasts pressed up against the hardness of his chest and her eyes rose to his in surprise, her hands landing on his pecs, confirming the muscle beneath her fingers.

Liam stared at her lips, his blue eyes darkening to midnight as he did. "You can't say words like wet to me, especially in that honey-dipped voice, treacle."

"I cannot? Why?"

"Because it makes me think about things I shouldn't be. Like how wet you might be if I dipped my fingers under the waistband of these trousers."

Her heart began to beat a rapid tattoo in her chest as excitement thrummed through her body, having the exact effect he was suggesting. "Oh," she murmured.

Liam smirked as if he could somehow tell what he was doing to her. "So, unless you want me to do that, I suggest we table talk of wet or moist things, and you stop walking around looking like fucking temptation."

Taamira paused, considering his words. The fact was, she did want him to do those things but to say she wasn't scared of the effect he had on her, and the ability he had to arouse her body, would be an understatement. Taamira bit her lip not knowing what to say.

Liam groaned. "Treacle, are you trying to kill me?

"No, of course not, and I wasn't trying to be a temptation."

"I know that, treacle. But with you looking like you do, and being the person you are and having you in my space, it's enough to make me want to break every rule in the book and say fuck it and let the chips land where they do."

Taamira liked his words and how they gave her confidence, as if she were beautiful and worthy.

"Shall we order in?"

Liam grinned and released her with a squeeze to her hip that was more of a caress. "Menus are in the third draw down on the left, Princess."

Taamira watched him walk towards his office before he turned his head back to her. "I have to make some calls. Just order whatever you want and get me the same."

She watched him disappear and turned to the drawer, and for the first time in her life, she was going to order food for another person. She found she liked the idea of taking care of someone; especially when that person was Liam.

CHAPTER ELEVEN

Liam pushed himself through one more set of goblet squats before he lowered the weight and wiped his face with a towel. He'd swapped out with Blake and Decker early this morning. He knew the Princess slept late after taking a sleeping pill, just one more thing he knew about her that perhaps he shouldn't. His attraction to her was becoming increasingly difficult to ignore, but more than that, so was the reason for it.

Watching her in his home last night as she puttered around his kitchen, she had seemed a world away from the Princess that was demanding and haughty. She had been sweet, listening to him, taking an interest in his home, his past. Ordering him food. Although thinking of that had him smiling inwardly.

He'd forgotten Taamira was who she was and in doing so had let down his guard, which was why he'd ended up with a fridge full of leftover Chinese food when she'd ordered enough for a banquet. It was also why he'd needed to escape, clear his mind, and use exercise to maintain his focus.

Last night he'd been so close to kissing her, to taking her hand and leading her to his bedroom and making her his in every way possible.

Only her innocence had stopped him, and even that almost wasn't enough when she looked at him as if she wanted to eat him.

She'd laughed, her eyes widening when the food was delivered, and she had realised how much food she'd bought. Liam had found it endearing, especially when she had tried to brazen it out by saying she was hungry and then tried to eat all of it. He'd sat back in his chair and grinned as she ate slower and slower, each mouthful becoming torturous before he'd taken pity on her, laughing, and taking the plate away.

Taamira had flopped her head on the table and groaned. "I am so full. I may never eat ever again."

Liam had cleared away their plates and packed away the food into containers in the fridge. "I forgot you're pampered, Princess. I should've ordered the food." He'd not meant anything by it, but when she went silent, he'd looked over and seen the hurt on her face.

"I cannot help how I was raised any more than anyone else can, but I am willing to learn new things, experience change, which is more than some can say."

Liam crossed to stand by her chair, lifting her chin with two fingers, so her gaze met his. "I'm sorry, treacle, I didn't mean anything by it."

"I know you did not, but it is dawning on me how much of the real world I have never seen. How different I am from everyone else, and I do not like it. I sometimes wish with all my heart that I was born into a normal family. That I could have gone to college to become whatever I wanted to be."

He'd looked at her and his chest tightened painfully at the melancholy look in her dark eyes. "I think everyone goes through that at some point. Sometimes more than once. I know I was lost for a long time when Ambrose died. I didn't know if I was in the right job, the right country, the right life."

"How did you find your way?"

Liam took a seat beside her. "My friends stood by me. Not just Eidolon, but Zack, Zin, Nate, Skye, Celeste, Pax, and now Callie. In fact, the girls were the best. They offered me a different perspective than the guys. Showed me it was okay to grieve and to take time to find my path."

"They seem very wise."

"They are pains in my ass, but I love them dearly. It's like having lots of little sisters. I'll see if we can arrange for you to meet them while we're here."

It was seeing the joy on her face that he realised how deep he was getting, because he could see himself falling for this woman.

The door to the gym opened, and Alex walked in.

The Cuban saw him and headed over. "Spot me?" he asked, pointing to the bench.

"Sure." Liam waited as Alex warmed up and had settled himself before he stood behind him. "Any word from Bás or Gunner?" Liam asked, wondering if they were any closer to having an answer on who the real threat to them was.

Alex's jaw tightened at the question. Bás was an unknown entity, and nobody was clear on who he was or where his loyalties really lay. Liam suspected they were with himself, but at this point, they had little choice but to work with him. Alex had a particular grudge against Bás, who'd been going by another name at the time, had tortured Evelyn, his fiancée and lost love.

"Nothing so far but Lopez is tracking Gunner, who is doing everything he said he was going to."

"Well, we do have his sister, so he has an incentive to cooperate," Liam pointed out.

"True and we don't know what Bás' weak spot is, or even if that's a name he goes by. Will hasn't found him, and that means this fucker is so deep he probably can't remember his own name."

"It's gonna be a long game."

Alex grunted as he lifted the bar, sweat rolling down his arms. "Talking of which, what's going on with you and the Princess?"

Liam tensed at the question, his back snapping straight. "Nothing's going on."

"You sure about that? Certainly looked like something to me."

"She trusts me is all."

"And you?"

"Fuck, Alex, what is this?" Liam bit out as Alex swung his legs around and sat up.

"Are you fucking her?"

"No, I'm not fucking her, and I object to the accusation." Liam paced angrily, guilty that he'd wanted to fuck her and indignation that Alex thought so little of him combining.

"Just an observation."

"As a boss or a friend?"

Alex shrugged. "Both."

"Well as a friend, fuck you and mind your own goddamn business, and as a boss, then no, sir, I'm being a good little boy."

Alex stood then, and glared at Liam. He was a couple of inches taller than him, but Liam was fucking furious.

"You've never wanted me as a boss," Alex snapped.

Liam stayed silent for a second because it was the truth, but not because he had anything against Alex. He was a great operator, fantastic guy, and good leader. The calm to Jack's storm. The fact was, Liam resented that he had taken Ambrose's place and that would have been the same for anyone. It made no sense, it was unfair, but it was what it was.

Liam was angry now though and let rip when he should have bit his tongue. "You're right, I don't want you as a boss. You're not half the man Ambrose was or half the leader," Liam bellowed.

"Glad we understand each other, brother," Alex snapped and walked towards the door before he turned back. "Just remember this, you're not the only person who lost a friend when Ambrose died. We all miss him, but some of us don't go around blaming the fucking world and burying ourselves in pity. Some of us have been through similar pain you have and come out the other side, learned to embrace what we do have, not what we lost."

With that, Alex walked out leaving Liam with a bucket load of guilt and regret. But, also with a realisation that perhaps he had wronged Alex and maybe his other friends.

His phone buzzed, and Blake's name lit up the screen. Liam sighed, wanting a few minutes to get his shit together before the next drama hit, he rubbed his eyes, tired to his bones the last few days. Instead, he answered. "Yeah."

"We have a situation."

"What now?"

"Taamira got a call, freaked out, locked herself in her room, and won't talk to us."

Liam was walking to the door as Blake spoke, urgency in his step. "What number did it come in on?"

"Her personal mobile."

"Do we know who from?" Liam slid into his truck, still in his gym gear as he questioned Blake.

"No, she won't give us the phone to check. All I know is she was trying to make tea in the kitchen when the call came. She took it before we could stop her and went very pale before she ran to her room and locked the door."

"Don't fucking leave her alone. Lock my doors and secure the grounds. If anyone traced the call, they may locate where she is."

Liam hung up and pressed his foot to the accelerator, taking the corners faster than he should. He slammed his hand on the horn when a tractor tried to pull out and overtook him to the sound of horns blaring.

He should've checked to see if she'd had a mobile. He hadn't, and that was on him, but by God, he wouldn't make any more mistakes.

He swerved into his drive five minutes later and was out of the vehicle before he'd completely stopped. He marched to his door, ignoring Digby, and was met by Blake and Decker.

"She in her room?" Decker nodded, and the two men went to follow, so he took a moment to stop and turn back to them. "I want a bug put on Prince Abdul's phone. I don't care how we do it, but I want it done."

"On it," Blake said, lifting his phone, no doubt to call Will. Lopez was good, very good, but Will, Jack's brother, was a fucking genius with technology.

"Deck, can you run me a profile? I want to know what type of person would go after the Princess in this way. Who the threats may be. My mark is the brother, but in case I'm missing something, can you put one together for me?"

"Yes, I can do that, but it'll be basic until we know more. Finding out who that was, or at least what they said, would give us more information."

"Will do."

Liam stopped at her door and took a deep breath to calm himself. He was desperate to see she was okay, but he needed to remain the calm one and not let her see he was freaking out. "Treacle, it's me. Open up the door." He knocked loudly and waited what seemed endless minutes for her to answer.

When she opened the door, and he saw the beautiful tearstained face and the look of despair in her eyes, he did the only thing he could. He leaned in and took her in his arms and held her tight.

CHAPTER TWELVE

TAAMIRA HAD NOT MEANT to fall apart, she had tried her hardest to keep it together but the words the caller had said opened up memories of the threats she had received and her fear for those she loved. It had been silly to run from Blake and Decker, but she couldn't seem to articulate what the person on the phone had said. When Liam knocked on the door, the sound of his voice had released a tsunami, and she'd fallen into his embrace.

He'd held her so tight, the scent of sweat, the heat of his body, as well as the muscled arms that always seemed to keep her safe had become a haven for her. It was the gentle look he'd settled on her, the soft words, and the way he had stroked her hair and not rushed her to tell him what had happened, that had her calm enough to speak.

"Let's sit." He led her to the large double bed and sat her down, before taking a seat next to her, not letting go of her hands. "Tell me what happened."

His body seemed relaxed, but over the months she had come to know this man better than she realised and his voice gave away his anger.

"Are you angry with me?"

Liam frowned. "Whatever for?"

Taamira worried her fingers, picking at her cuticles and not looking him in the eye. She hated this meek side of herself, wished she could be the confident woman she portrayed for the world instead of the girl cowed by domineering men. Liam placed his hand over hers to still her movements.

"Taamira, why would I be angry?" His voice was firmer now but in no way cruel.

"I panicked and shut myself away. I should have talked to Blake and Decker and told them what happened instead of dragging you back here."

"You have nothing to be sorry for, fear is a cruel mistress. Nobody should be made to feel bad for it. Tell me what happened."

"I was pouring the tea when my phone rang. I recognised the number as my niece Najwa. I haven't heard from her in so long, and I was excited to speak with her. But when I answered it was a distorted male voice."

Taamira frowned at the memory and gripped Liam's fingers harder in her own. Sensing her discord, he lifted his arm and pulled her against his chest, resting his chin on her head. Knowing she was safe, she continued. "He said I was a disgrace to my people and that if I didn't stop my public engagements and decline the invitation to speak at the conference then Najwa and my other niece would be raped and the videos leaked online." Her voice shook as she said the last, the threat of that act perpetrated on her teenage nieces so horrific she could hardly bear it.

Liam stilled to an almost statue at her words. Pulling back, she looked up into his face and saw pure fury. If it had been any other man, she would have run, but she knew his ire wasn't directed at her but at the person who had threatened her.

"Where is your phone now?"

Taamira rose and went to get it from the dresser where she had dropped it. Picking it up, she saw her hand was shaking and took a deep breath as she tried to control it. Returning to him, she dropped it into his outstretched hand.

"Who had this number?" he asked as he opened it and scrolled through her meagre contacts.

"Just my nieces. They are the only ones who have any kind of affection for me now."

"Are they likely to have given it to anyone else?"

"No, they are loyal." She shook her head with vehemence. That gave her pause though because if someone had made the threat, then they could very well have hurt Najwa.

She gripped his arm tightly. "Liam, we must make sure she is okay."

"I'll have someone put out some feelers to see if we can find out if they're safe."

Taamira nodded and then looked sadly out of the window at Digby. "I must make a call to the conference organisers and cancel my speech."

"No way."

Taamira swung her gaze back to Liam, who was prowling towards her slowly. "But I must. If I do not, then my nieces will suffer. Liam, you do not understand. If they make good on the threat, not only would they suffer from the act itself and the shame, but they would be forced to marry the perpetrator or risk death at the hands of a male family member because of the shame it would bring to the family."

Liam's face twisted into a look she could not read and didn't want to before he wiped his face into a neutral expression. "That is the very reason, Princess, that you need to make your speech and fight to get the laws changed. It should never be okay for a woman who has been attacked to become the person in the wrong. No woman should face the fear or threat of such a heinous act being held against them and they should never, in any way, be made to believe they're to blame."

He reached up and gently cupped her cheeks. "You were right

the other night to fight for your right to make that speech. You have the voice these women need, and we'll find a way for them to hear you. We won't rest until we make changes that, at the very least, allow women to feel safe from crimes against them."

"We?" she asked, hope blooming in her chest for the first time since the call came in.

"We," he reiterated as he held her gaze. "We're friends, and I'll do whatever it takes to help you and protect you, and in the process, protect them."

Taamira's shoulders sagged a little at his words, her chest aching which was silly. This incredible man was offering to help her make the lives of her female counterparts safer, and she was a horrible person for letting disappointment enter her head. Yet, at the word friend, her heart had fallen. She wanted so much more from this man who believed in her, more than anyone ever had, who seemed always to support her and keep her safe.

A cockney boy from the Eastend he called himself, and yet he carried himself and held himself to account better than any King she had ever known and that included her father, who until his abandonment, she had loved very much.

"You are a good man, Liam Hayes. A king among men."

Liam stroked his thumb over her cheek gently before he blushed and let go. "I'm just doing what any friend would do."

That word again. He used it as a shield, and for a moment she wondered who he was trying to remind—her or himself.

CHAPTER THIRTEEN

As TAAMIRA SHOWERED, Liam moved through to his home office. It was a large room that overlooked the back paddock. He rarely used it, as he preferred to be around his friends, but he liked to sit there and watch the world in peace sometimes. The large glass desk was tidy, only holding his laptop with a secured VPN, an empty notebook, and a coaster.

Thinking of his friends had him turning to his conversation with Alex. He had been entirely out of order with the man. Alex had never been anything other than a friend to him, and if he were honest, he knew he'd been selfish. He was not the only person who'd lost a friend the day Ambrose died, yet he'd behaved like he was.

He now recognised it must have been incredibly hard for Alex to step up and he'd done a fantastic job. Liam owed Alex, and probably the others, a massive apology. He took out his phone and toyed with the idea of calling, but that was a pussy thing to do. Alex deserved a proper apology in person. Which would have to wait until later, or even tomorrow, depending on how the day panned out.

His phone on his desk rang, and he saw Jack's name so he answered. "Boss."

"I'm at the gate."

"I'll let you in, come on up."

After they had arrived home yesterday, Liam had closed the main gate at the bottom of his drive. It was far from bombproof, but it allowed him to see if anyone approached the property.

Moving to the front door, he unlocked it remotely and waited for Jack to pull up. His boss parked facing the exit, ready to move if he needed to. Jack swung from the car, his sunglasses covering his eyes. He strode towards him, not giving anything away as to why he was here.

Liam stepped back and allowed his boss entrance. "Want to go through to the office?"

Jack nodded and slipped his glasses from his face.

Liam followed, wondering if he was about to get fired for the way he'd spoken to Alex. He closed the door and faced Jack. "If this is about the way I spoke to Alex, then I already know I've been a dick. I'll apologise the first chance I get, but it needs to be done in person."

Jack lifted his chin. "Good, because you were a giant dickhead."

"I know." Liam shoved his hands in his pockets. "Did Alex tell you?"

"Of course not. Alex isn't a fucking grass. He's a good man and a good friend. He stepped up when we lost Ambrose, and it was hard for him."

Jack sat down in the office chair and looked up at Liam. "Not as hard as it was for you, we all recognise that. But every person on this team has their own shit going on, and you need to recognise that and understand we're a unit. If one bleeds, we all bleed."

Liam leaned his ass against the desk, his hands gripping the edge at Jack's words. "How did you know?"

"I saw it on the camera. If you ask me, you're lucky Alex didn't deck you."

Liam chuckled. "I guess."

"Listen, all I'm saying is it's okay to grieve for your friend but honour his memory by being the man he knew, not someone who turns on his friends, because Ambrose would've been the first to kick your ass for that."

Liam knew Jack was right, and he had some serious soul searching to do and some amends to make. "I guess I have some grovelling to do."

"No, just stop being a twat, that's all." Jack looked out the window at Digby and shook his head with a grin. "Bet she loved him."

Liam knew exactly who he meant. "Oh, she sure did. Thinks he's cute."

"Huh." Jack glanced his way. "How's she doing?"

"Okay. She was doing well after the attempt in Madrid, but this call shook her up."

"I bet it did, and that's why I'm here. My contact confirmed that both her nieces are fine and healthy and show no signs of harm."

The air left Liam's lungs in a whoosh. "Thank fuck. It would kill her if anything happened to them."

Jack eyed him carefully. "You're falling for her."

Liam's instinct was to deny it, but he honestly needed someone to tell him to step away. "I didn't see it coming but yes. I haven't done anything about it. Taamira is so far out of my league, she's practically a different species."

"Maybe, but I have a feeling it's mutual. Taamira won't hear of anyone else taking care of her security. You make her feel safe and seen, and I think that's something she hasn't had in a long time."

"Makes no difference, does it? This ain't a fairy tale, and I'm no prince charming."

"You can fucking say that again, you ugly fucker." Jack chuckled. "But I think safety and security and someone who can see the real person behind the title is exactly what she needs."

Liam stayed quiet on that front and knew he would absorb it later. Liam crossed his arms over his chest. "So, this means whoever called has access to the niece's phone."

"Yes. I have Lopez compiling a list of every person who has

access to them in any way. That way we can narrow down the suspects based on the profile Decker is running."

"And Hassan?"

Jack's lip curled. "Low-level merchant that works in the market outside the palace. He was offered money by some unseen person to carry out the attack."

"A dead-end then."

"Not exactly. Depends if we can keep him in play somehow. He gave up his contact point so we might be able to use that."

"Is Mitch heading that up?"

"Yeah, him and Waggs."

"I need to see the guestlist for the conference and the plans for the building. I don't want any risks I can't mitigate when she goes on that stage."

"Come in tomorrow and I'll have it ready. Stay close to home today until she settles."

Jack stood as they heard Taamira moving about downstairs. "I'll say a quick hello and then leave you to it."

Liam followed him out, but Jack turned back to him. "Remember what I said. What you think she needs isn't necessarily the same as what she actually needs. My opinion, for what it's worth, is that you need each other." He patted Liam on the shoulder. "On that, I'm going back to being a grumpy asshole and closing my column as an agony aunt. So if you need anything else, ask Decker."

Liam grinned and watched as Jack went to speak with Taamira. She smiled and greeted Jack like a friend, even hugging him. Liam kept his distance, but he saw the gentleness Jack handled her with and the way she responded and thought maybe Jack was right about them needing each other.

He hadn't been able to let her out of his sight all day. Not because she was clingy in any way but because he couldn't bear to leave her as Jack's words played over and over in his head.

Taamira had pulled herself together surprisingly well. Once he'd convinced her to carry on with the conference, she'd used his secure phone in the office to make some calls to the heads of her charity, conducting business remotely.

He'd watched her discreetly as she did, noticing the way she played with her hair, laughed freely, and asked about their families before she got down to business. She made them feel like they mattered to her. She had a way about her that was inborn, maybe it was her royalty, but he didn't think so—it was a Taamira thing.

It was nearing dinner time now, and he already had the mince out to make spaghetti Bolognese. She didn't know it yet, but Taamira was about to get a cooking lesson. He smiled as he thought about teaching her new things, then promptly stopped his thoughts as his mind went in a totally inappropriate direction.

The issue he had was he liked her; he didn't just want to fuck her and discover her sweet spots. He loved spending time with her. If he were honest, he had from the beginning, ever since she'd looked at his flowered holiday shirt with disdain.

High maintenance women had always drawn him. He liked them feisty and full of attitude, and Taamira's demands had only intrigued him more. Despite letting everyone think it annoyed him, the way she demanded he attend to her turned him on.

But as they spent more time together and he saw her sweet side, the way she cared about people and things, his feelings became more complex. He was getting in deep with this woman, and he knew he shouldn't because he couldn't be what she needed.

Taamira needed a man that was cultured and well-spoken. Who knew which damn spoon to use for a shrimp cocktail, not a man who ate sushi with a fork because chopsticks were a pain in the ass. Jack's reasoning that she needed security stuck in his head, though.

As he moved towards the back door to feed Digby his last meal of the day, Taamira walked into the kitchen. She was wearing tight blue jeans that had been driving him crazy all day with the way they hugged her ass, an olive-green vee neck cashmere jumper, and flat grey boots. It was hard to keep the barrier in place seeing her in regular clothes, especially when his gut clenched at how she looked so effortlessly beautiful.

"Where are you going?"

"It's time for Digby's dinner. Want to help me?"

He wanted to take her in his arms at the way her face lit up with eagerness.

"Yes, please."

Liam grinned and held the door for her to go through ahead of him.

As they walked to the wooden shed in the corner of the garden where he kept Digby's feed for ease of access, he couldn't help admiring her ass, or the sexy sway of her hips.

"What does he eat?" Taamira asked as she pulled her hair from her face only for it to blow back.

She looked so gorgeous he wanted to kiss her, to take her face between his hands and taste the berry lips.

"Liam?"

Her voice brought him out of his fantasy. "Oh yeah, feed. He has barley, straw, and grass mainly but because he's older and to keep his weight up, I feed him additional high fibre pellets. He occasionally gets apples, carrots, swedes, that kind of thing but that's only as a treat."

Liam filled the bucket with feed and looked up to see Digby running towards them. Closing the shed, they walked towards the gate.

"Oh, what a beautiful boy." Taamira was stroking the animal's soft ears and cooing over him as Digby lapped it up, nuzzling her jumper.

"Come on, Digby," Liam said as he shook the bucket into the trough.

With food on offer, the donkey quickly abandoned Taamira. Liam came to stand beside her, stroking the animal's back as he did.

"Do you know how old he is?"

Liam shook his head. "Not really but the vet thinks around twenty-two."

Once they had finished feeding and settling Digby, Liam led them back inside. "I was going to make spaghetti Bolognese for dinner. Would you like to learn how?"

Taamira smiled. "You are willing to share one of your four recipes with me?"

"As long as you do the dishes."

Her face lit up at something that would usually be met by groaning in any other person. "Deal. Let me wash up and I will be right back."

Liam grinned as he washed his own hands. His phone buzzed in his pocket, and he took it out and read the message. Decker had a basic profile for him but would give him something more detailed by tomorrow.

Liam clicked the link he'd sent and read through it. There were no surprises in it really, but it was good to have. In his opinion, it still pointed towards her brother though. He tucked the phone away as Taamira came back into the kitchen.

"Any more news on my nieces?"

He saw her eyes move to his pocket and realised she'd been keeping busy to distract herself from going crazy with worry.

"Nothing more yet, but at least we know they're safe for now. Jack will call as soon as he hears anything else." He had seen her relief when Jack had given her the news that her nieces were unharmed as far as they could tell.

Taamira nodded and then forced a smile that didn't reach her eyes. He hated that, he wanted to see the joy, the happiness that reached her soul.

"Have you ever cooked before?" he asked instead as she moved closer to him, her scent enveloping him.

"Not really."

Her embarrassment was cute, so he grinned. "Then this is a nice easy one to start with."

They worked together side by side as Liam showed her how to brown the turkey mince which he had swapped out with his regular beef, knowing Taamira didn't eat beef, pork, or lamb, not liking the taste of red meats. He found it was fun to cook with someone else, and she was a quick study. Before long they had the Bolognese simmering and the pasta on to boil.

"That was easier than I thought. I wonder what else we can make?"

The light was back in her eyes, and he liked it. He moved so she was up against the counter and pinned her with his hands either side. The last hour as they cooked had driven him to the edge of what he could take. He wanted her so badly, and surely one taste wouldn't hurt. It would probably help get her out of his system he rationalised.

"You make me burn with the need to taste you," he admitted, watching her eyes go wide before her gaze settled on his lips.

His head descended, and the last thing he saw were her eyes fluttering closed before his lips touched hers, and he realised one taste would never be enough.

CHAPTER FOURTEEN

DRUGGED—THAT was the only way to describe the feeling as Liam kissed her. It wasn't a light brush of the lips, but neither was it an all-out assault. She wanted to melt into his body, the kiss was firm, probing, and languid. Her hands moved to his chest, the electric touch of his fingers along her hips causing goose bumps to pepper her skin. He didn't push, but he led her where he seemed to know she needed to go.

Then it was gone, and she was looking into his sky-blue eyes. They held heat, passion, but also surprise and a little of something else she couldn't put her finger on. Her hands still rested on his chest, which flexed beneath her fingers.

Liam blew out a breath which feathered along her skin before he stepped back. "I'm sorry."

"Please do not say that. It makes me think you regret it and I could not feel further from that."

She stayed still as he moved to the pasta, stirring it as if to give his hands something to do. He glanced at her as he laid the spoon aside, then took her hand and pulled her towards the kitchen table.

"Take a seat, Princess."

Taamira did, and he sat beside her, not letting her fingers go. The simple gesture of her hand in his, with no sexual overtones was intimate, giving her security and warmth.

"I have no doubt that I'm not good enough for you, as a friend or anything more." She went to object, but he stopped as he looked into her face, a schoolboy grin on his face. "Let me finish, treacle."

Taamira snapped her mouth closed and cherished the grin he gave her as her heart beat faster.

"The thing is, even knowing this, I can't stop thinking about how good we could be together. I don't even know if I'm reading this all wrong and you have no inclination of a romantic involvement with me at all. But if you do, then I want to try."

Taamira waited to see if he'd finished as he remained looking at her. He began to fidget adorably, and she found it even more endearing. This man was something of a conundrum to her; one minute he was confident and took charge, the next when it came to affairs of the heart, he was unsure of himself. In that way, they were very similar.

Taamira took his face in her palms, the stubble on his cheeks bristling against her skin. "We are not so different, you and I. We are both unsure in the realms of romance, me because of my sheltered upbringing and you," Taamira paused, "perhaps not in the physical sense but in the relationship side of things, you have not been so lucky."

Heat tinged Taamira's cheeks and she was glad for her darker skin tone to mask it. Liam grinned though as if sensing her discomfort and she frowned at him in mock annoyance. "You are laughing at me."

"No, Princess, not laughing at you. I find it cute how you blush at any mention of sex." He leaned closer and ran his thumb along her bottom lip, her breath hitching in her chest, which he also noticed. "Makes me want to see if the heat touches your skin all over your body."

Heat flooded her body at his words, ripples of desire moving through her and landing in her belly.

"But you're right, I've had my fair share of sexual partners, but I've never been in love, never wanted forever and while I'm not saying that's what I want now, it is the closest I've come to wanting that. You're the first person to make me believe I could have that. Which is crazy, you're a fucking princess and I'm nobody."

"You are a somebody, and to me, you are somebody special. How about we take this slow and see how it develops? You may find that I am an annoyance that you cannot be bothered with, and I may find you are an irritating oaf."

Liam hooked her around her waist, pulling her so that she was sitting on his lap, her bottom on his hard thighs. "Irritating oaf?" he asked with a lift of his dark eyebrow.

She liked this playful side of him, almost as much as she loved his kisses. "Why, yes."

"Hmm, seems like the Princess wants to play."

Her body heated at his tone of voice. Taamira was a virgin, had barely been kissed, but that didn't mean she was not unlike any other woman. She had desires, she had fantasies, and more than a few involved this man.

They were face to face as he leaned in and kissed her again, parting her lips gently with his tongue. The firm softness of his lips, the taste of him gave her a thrill all the way down her body to her pussy. His hand cupped her face, tilting her head so he had her exactly where he wanted her, and she sank into it. Letting herself feel every second, allowing her passion to be free, her hands moved over his shoulders, digging into the muscles of his back.

Liam slowed the kiss, pulling back and dropping tiny pecks on her neck and cheeks before he gazed at her again. "You'll never be an annoyance to me, Taamira. Not fucking ever."

Tears stung the backs of her eyes at his words, burning her throat at she allowed the emotion of the moment to take hold. For the first time in her life, she was important for herself. Not her title, not her place in society, not her money but simply because of who she was.

They spent the rest of the night eating a dinner they had cooked together and was one of her favourite meals in the world now. After she had washed and dried the dishes, they moved to the living room, where a fifty-two-inch TV graced the wall. As she snuggled into Liam's side and watched an action movie, she had never been more content.

Later that night as she was readying for bed alone, after a passionate kiss at her door, which once again, Liam had ended, she considered what they were embarking on. Was it foolish to start a relationship with Liam when she had not outlined the rules with him? Did he expect sex from her, and did she want that too? To say she had lapsed her traditions was an understatement, for she did not think she could believe in them when they did not allow women the same rights as men.

Yet, her cultural rules had got her through some difficult times in her life. Giving her the structure she needed to become who she was now. But picking and choosing what rules she followed for her gain was wrong.

What she needed was to study the history and rules she had followed her entire life and see if they still fit with who she was now. She had changed almost beyond her own recognition and did not see how those values fit her any longer.

Going to her bed, she slipped inside the sheets and lifted her diary from the bedside. Writing had been part of her life since the attack when she'd been cast aside by her family for crimes against her. When she had visited her family elders, they had told her she needed to pray for forgiveness, and that single sentence had a lasting impact on how she had regarded her culture.

That was not to say all of her people would have said that, but at a time when she needed support, she had found only rejection. Gravely wounded, she had all but abandoned her culture but now she needed to find out of it was still a part of her or not.

Her confusion mixed up her desire for Liam, but not just desire. Her feelings for him grew ever more complicated by the day. He was fast becoming everything to her. For that reason, she had to decide where she thought her future might lie.

CHAPTER FIFTEEN

THE LAST FIVE days had been hectic, to say the least, and as Liam pulled up at the hangar for his flight to Geneva, he hated leaving Taamira. Their relationship, which even thinking it sounded crazy, was going well.

They were taking things incredibly slowly, and that was as much him as it was her. He wanted her more than he had ever wanted anything in his life, each night ended with him jerking off in the shower as he thought about varying scenarios featuring the woman who drove him crazy. But he wanted her to be sure before she gave him something she couldn't get back.

Her being a virgin was something he both loved and hated, loved because he wanted to be her first, hated because of the responsibility it gave him. They hadn't discussed it, but it also went against her traditions to have sex before marriage, and although he knew Taamira wasn't as led by her culture as some were, he knew she still struggled with the guilt from her very strict upbringing.

Perhaps being away would allow him some relief from the constant desire she awoke in him. Then maybe they should have a conversation before the kisses and make-out sessions went too far.

As he climbed the steps to the private jet he would be taking, Liam glanced at the pilot and hated that he missed Gunner. The man had been beside him for many missions, and not having him as the pilot still irked. The man had kept his word so far though and was feeding back small titbits of information that while meant nothing in isolation, put together they began to form a picture they all hoped would help them find the real threat behind the masks.

He slid into the seat and buckled his seatbelt but glanced up as he saw movement on the steps. His gaze locked with Alex, who also paused. The two hadn't had a chance to work through their differences, although to call it that was unfair to Alex. The blame lay squarely at Liam's feet.

Alex came to sit beside him, the atmosphere awkward at best as he secured his belt. The engine came to life, and before long, they were in the air. Not wanting it to continue any longer and knowing he had to make the first move to fix what he had broken, Liam angled towards, Alex.

"I reckon I owe you an apology."

Alex looked him dead in the eyes and said nothing; he was obviously going to make Liam work for his forgiveness.

"You were right. I've behaved like a complete asshole. I was making Ambrose's death about me when it wasn't. We all lost him, and I failed to recognise that. I'm sorry, you're the only person who could've stepped into his shoes, and you filled them. I guess in part that's what hurt. Life went on, and I didn't."

Alex nodded, and grinned. "You're off the hook, mate."

Liam sighed. "Thank God."

Alex chuckled, then sobered. "For what it's worth, I do get it. You had a history we never did, and it was always going to be harder for you. But I truly believe he wouldn't want this for you."

"Ambrose would've kicked my sorry ass."

"He would, and then we would've headed to the Red Lion and he'd have bought us all a pint."

"Yeah, he would."

Alex rested his hands on the armrest and leaned back. "For what it's worth, I never meant that Taamira was too good for you. I was worried it might be fun for you, but now, after a butt-kicking from my fiancée for meddling, I can see it's way more than that."

"Siren beat you up?"

Liam smirked, knowing that the love between Alex and Evelyn, aka Siren, was immeasurable. He adored her and she adored him and any ass-kicking was metaphorical.

"Let's just say she showed me the error of my ways." Alex grinned, and it hid a thousand secrets that Liam had no interest in knowing, but it did make him smile inwardly.

Alex having Evelyn had strengthened his friend he saw that, it was the same with Blake and Pax. Each couple seemed to round each other out, accentuate their strengths and bolster their weaknesses. Is that what he could expect from Taamira if they moved forward and by some miracle she didn't come to her senses and see him for what he was?

Liam sobered as he thought of Alex's words. It was easy to see why people would think he wasn't serious and only wanted a hook-up. Before her, that would have been true, it would have been about mutual satisfaction. Now though, he knew he had a precious treasure in his hands and there was no way he would fumble it.

"You're right, though, she is too good for me, but by some strange act of fate she doesn't think so."

"See, just that sentence shows how worthy you are. When you love someone, especially a woman, you spend every day feeling as if you're not good enough, because she makes you want to be better than before in every single way and that never ends."

"Is that how Evelyn makes you feel?" Liam asked, knowing he was perhaps overstepping.

Alex chuckled. "Every day of my life I wonder what I did to deserve her, and I still have no fucking clue."

"Sounds like I'm in good company."

"Does she know how you feel about her?"

Liam shrugged. "We talked, said we were going to take it day by day, but honestly, I'm not sure where it's headed. I've never really thought long term before."

"And now you are?"

"I guess. I don't know. I mean, how could it work? She's a damn princess, and I'm a nobody."

"You might see it that way, but others don't. To those that give a fuck about you, it matters—you matter."

Liam went silent as he thought over his friend's words which only led to more confusion, so he blocked it from his mind and gave some thought to the security breach back in Madrid.

Lopez was running in-depth background checks on the two they had identified as the most likely candidates. Until the investigation wrapped, they'd been stood down with full pay. As soon as he had those checks, he could figure out how to move forward with Taamira's security. Although right now, the only people he trusted were Eidolon.

That was the reason he'd left her at home with Blake and Pax as house guests. Blake had in-depth experience with Royalty having been the Personal Protection Officer for the Queen at one time. Still, he wanted to get to the venue, check it over, and get home.

Once on the ground, he and Alex caught a cab to the venue, which was a large hotel with a massive conference room. Just the fact it was a hotel offered so many risks; his chest squeezed like he might have a heart attack from the very thought. Every instinct in his body told him to make her pull out from this speech. But then he remembered the look on her face and what it meant to her, and he couldn't do it.

He and Alex spent hours with the hotel security team going over every possible eventuality. They had agreed to meet in the morning and go over the guestlist for the three days before the event and then walk the entire building and grounds again looking for possible problems for the security team.

Which was another headache Liam had because he now had fewer options since Derek's team were off rotation.

"I don't like how thin we'll be on the ground," Liam said to Alex as they ate a quick dinner of spaghetti and meatballs.

Alex chewed slowly as he thought. "What about Fortis? Zack might be able to help and send a few guys."

"I'm gonna call him after dinner."

They ate in companionable silence for a while before Liam chucked the company credit card down and paid the bill. That taken care of, he walked to the room he'd booked when it became clear he'd have to stay over. He'd sent texts to Taamira a few times today and had waited with bated breath like a lovesick teen watching the dots dance as she'd replied.

One thing he was learning about the woman who was working her way into his heart was that she had a wicked sense of humour. One of the many things he was learning since she'd opened up and shown him the real woman.

He dialled Zack's number first wanting to have that settled and if not, have time to find another option.

"What did you do now?" Was Zack's greeting.

Liam chuckled. "Nothing. I'm as pure as the driven snow."

"Like fuck you are." Zack laughed. "What can I do for you, Liam?"

"I have a situation and I could do with a few more bodies. Any chance we can borrow a few of your guys?"

"When and where?"

"Five days and in Geneva. Taamira is giving a speech."

"Yeah, I heard you had trouble with her team. Bloody assholes, can't trust anyone these days."

"I know and I checked them meticulously."

"Of course you did. You're one of the most finicky bastards I ever worked with and if I thought I could poach you permanently, I would."

Liam didn't know what to say to that, but it meant a lot to him.

He had done a lot of work with Fortis and Zack. He and his men were as close as the Eidolon team, and in fact, as agencies were on excellent terms and often socialised together.

"Can't say it's not a tempting offer but Eidolon is home, you know." He realised as he said it that it was true. He'd never recognised that until now, or perhaps he'd never actively acknowledged it.

"I do know that and respect it. I can probably spare four of my guys. How does me, Zin, K, and Dane sound?"

"Sounds perfect, thank you. I really appreciate it."

"I hear the Princess is making waves. Good for her. After what her family did, they should be fucking shot. I hope she makes enough fuss that the assholes drown in the media onslaught."

"I'm sure she would appreciate your support."

"Email me the details, and I'll work out logistics with Jack."

"I'll do that, and thanks, Zack."

"Anytime, Pyro."

"I'm never gonna live that down am I?"

"You did blow a fucking helo out of the sky, almost landing it on my building," Zack exclaimed with a sigh.

"It was for the greater good."

"My ass. You just wanted to show off your toys."

Liam laughed, they both knew the truth, and that was he had done what he had to save a lot of lives.

"You got me, Zack."

Zack laughed and hung up, and Liam's shoulders sagged. That was one problem solved. Hopefully, tomorrow they could iron out the rest as best they could. But everyone knew it was almost impossible to predict every given scenario, but he was going to do his damndest.

He was about to call Taamira when he got a text from Blake. It showed Taamira with Callie, Pax, and Evelyn sitting in his living room with glasses of something fizzy. The caption read, *meeting the natives.*

He shook his head and smiled. He was pleased that the girls were dragging Taamira into their little group. She hadn't had a lot of girlfriends she could trust from what he could make out. If there was one thing he knew, those three women would be loyal, and God help anyone who hurt someone they considered part of their girl squad.

As he climbed in the shower, deciding he would call Taamira later, he grinned happily. She was not only safe from physical harm, but with new friends and people who cared for her as a person around her, Taamira was safe, and that was all that mattered to him.

CHAPTER SIXTEEN

TAAMIRA HATED TO ADMIT IT, but she was missing Liam already. He'd only left that morning, and she already wanted to call him. When the first text came through, she couldn't help the grin that spread across her face. It had only been a meme from a movie, but as it was one they'd watched the other night, it had her smiling with delight.

She had taken full responsibility for feeding Digby when she heard Liam ask Mitch who had shown up with Blake earlier. Liam had chuckled and snagged her around the back of her neck, pulling her close for a sweet kiss that had her toes curling in her boots.

"You want to take care of my donkey then have it, treacle. You remember how much he has?"

Taamira nodded eagerly knowing she must seem silly to them. "Yes."

"Suits me, that mule hates me anyway." Mitch shrugged as he went inside the house behind Blake, who had just informed them Pax would be by later.

Taamira was uncharacteristically nervous at the thought of meeting Pax, and she found herself biting her lip.

Liam had sensed her anxiety, turned her, so she was facing him but still within the circle of his arms. "Talk to me."

"It's silly." Taamira dropped her eyes in embarrassment.

She had met Kings and Queens, super stars, and billionaires yet meeting a female friend of the man who was quickly becoming everything to her frightened her to death.

Liam lifted her chin with his finger, so she was looking him in the eye. "Nothing that makes you look like that is silly."

His words made her go gooey inside. "Liam," she said softly.

"I mean it. Now tell me," he demanded with firmness.

"Fine, I'm worried about meeting Pax."

His hard face softened. "Pax is the sweetest person. She may come across full of confidence, but she has her own story to tell. Trust me, Princess, I wouldn't put you in this position if I thought for one second you'd end up hurt in any way. But if you want me to tell Blake she should stay home, I will."

Taamira shook her head, heartened by his words. "No, I want to meet her. I'm just not used to being around women who don't have an agenda."

Liam laughed and raised an eyebrow. "Oh, she has an agenda."

Taamira stiffened. "She does?"

"Oh, yeah, to get as much information out of you as she can about us. These women are nosey mares."

Taamira wrinkled her nose. "I will not be telling her anything."

Liam kissed her forehead gently. "Good luck with that, Princess."

He had eased back and looked down at her, taking in every curve of her body or so it seemed. The heat in his eyes harder and harder for her to resist, and yet he had not pushed her in the slightest. In fact, it was always him who pulled back from their kissing sessions.

"Go in the house, treacle, or I may never leave."

She had done as he asked but watched from the window as he drove away. Now she had fed Digby and was going to ask Mitch and Blake if they wanted her to order some food. Both men were watching football in the living room and arguing good-naturedly about the teams and the poor referee who was getting lots of abuse from both of them.

The door rang, and she had been about to answer it when Blake had stopped her. The man was almost as bossy as Liam, insisting he go with her to feed Digby and now moving her away from the door and into the living room as he went to answer. Mitch was on his feet too, standing in front of her.

She heard him open it and then heard a flurry of female voices before the door to the lounge opened and Taamira looked at three of the most beautiful women she had ever seen.

"You must be Taamira," said a strikingly beautiful redhead who was holding a pan in her hand.

"Um, yes," she agreed as they all watched her.

The woman dropped into a simile of a curtsey which had Blake rolling his eyes.

"Babe, stop. This is embarrassing."

The woman glared at him and then pushed the pan into his hands. "Go put this in the oven, please."

Blake raised an eyebrow. "Is that how you greet me?"

The woman grinned and moved to him, raising on tiptoe and kissing him soundly on the mouth. "Better?" she asked as she wiped lipstick from his mouth.

"Much." Blake moved out of the room, and Mitch quickly followed, leaving her with the three women.

They all looked at each other for a second before they burst out laughing. "I told you we shouldn't descend en masse like this," said the tall blonde, who seemed familiar.

"Oh, behave, Callie. We just want to make friends," said the tiny brunette with the smile of a goddess.

The blonde ignored her and moved forward with her hand out. "I'm Callie Lund, it's nice to meet you..." She paused clearly, not knowing what to call her.

Taamira was always addressed as Your Royal Highness or

Princess Taamira, but to them, she didn't want to be that. These women were part of Liam's life in some way, and she wanted to be just Taamira. "Taamira, or Tami to my friends, so Tami I hope."

Callie grinned wide and shook her hand. "Nice to meet you, Tami. This here is Pax and Evelyn." She turned to the other two who stepped forward and greeted her the same way.

"Pax is with Blake as you could probably tell from the lip lock and Evelyn is engaged to Alex. I'm with Reid." Callie blushed as she said it and Taamira wondered if their relationship was quite new too.

"It's lovely to meet you," Taamira answered. "Would you like some tea?" She knew that tea was the customary offering in these social situations.

"No, thanks. I have this instead." Evelyn showed her a bottle of the fizzy apple and pear juice that Taamira loved, and she grinned at the woman.

"Liam told Alex who told me," Evelyn said with a twitch of her lips.

"I made Cajun Chicken Pasta for dinner," Pax added

Callie grinned and held up a bag. "And I have the fixings for cherry and almond cheesecake."

"Wow, this is..." Taamira had no words to show her appreciation.

These women didn't know her at all, and here they were offering her kindness and friendship. Taamira held back her glee, having a built in cautiousness from being burned in the past.

"Too much." Callie glared at her friends.

"No, no." Taamira held up her hand, not wanting them to think she was ungrateful. "It's very kind of you. Let's go through to the kitchen and pour the drinks."

Pax grinned, and Evelyn rolled her eyes.

Taamira led the way and soon had glasses on the table as Evelyn poured them all a glass.

"What about Blake and Mitch?" Taamira asked, looking around and wondering where the men had gone.

Pax waved a hand in the air as if that explained it all. "Oh, don't mind them, they'll be in the den watching football now."

Callie was pulling out ingredients for the cheesecake, and Pax was checking the pot she'd had Blake put in the oven. The smell of spices and cream hit her nose, and Taamira's tummy rumbled with hunger.

"That smells divine."

"It's a recipe I got off Pinterest. It's Blake's favourite, and I want a new pair of shoes, so..."

Taamira laughed at that piece of information.

"If you like the smell of that, this is going to blow your mind," Callie called as she went through the cupboards looking for a whisk.

"Can I help?" Taamira asked as Pax and Evelyn sat at the kitchen table with a glass of the juice.

Callie smiled. "Of course." She handed Taamira the whisk and showed her what to do, and opened a can of cherries.

"Liam mentioned you like to cook," Callie said.

Taamira glanced at her still thinking she looked familiar but not placing her. "I am learning, but at the moment I am very much a new foal."

"Me too. I never got the chance to eat a lot of dessert before now, what with the modelling but now I'm retired so I can eat whatever the hell I want." Callie popped a cherry into her mouth as she spoke.

"That's it, you're the model. I knew I recognised your face from somewhere."

"I was the model now I'm just a business-woman."

"What do you do?"

"Callie is a philanthropist," Pax added from her spot at the table.

"Really?" Taamira said, intrigued.

"Well, I've started a charity for models and girls who have eating disorders and addiction problems. It's very much in its infancy, so if you have any advice for me I'd really appreciate it."

"Oh, I would be delighted to help you in any way I can."

"Thank you."

The room was filled with chatter for the next thirty minutes as the three of them got to know her and she them. It was an experience she had never had before, and the more they shared stories of how they met the men they loved, the more Taamira relaxed. By the time the food was ready she felt like she had three new friends, the first she had ever had.

Pax had taken food through to Mitch and Blake who had said they were happy to sit in the den and eat so the girls could gossip.

Pax had laughed. "Gunmen and terrorists they can handle, but four women scares the crap out of them."

Taamira dug into her food and groaned at the first forkful. "Oh, this is amazing."

"I know, right. I love Pinterest. I get all my recipes on there."

"I have not heard of it," Taamira replied, and all three women looked at her.

"No way. Pinterest is like the black hole. It sucks you in for hours and then spits you back out full of new recipes and home decoration ideas."

"And hot pics of men," Evelyn added with a laugh which had the other two joining in.

"Can you show me after dinner?" Taamira asked shyly.

It was not strange to her that she was the odd one out, she had spent her life that way, but it was nice not to have it make her so vulnerable.

"Yes, of course. Let's leave the cleaning up and go through to the lounge with our cheesecake, and we can get the laptop out," Evelyn added.

As the night wore on, Taamira relaxed more and laughed at the images the girls showed her of men, the blush of innocence creeping over her cheeks. What she did not feel was like an outsider.

"So, tell us about you and Liam?" Pax asked and received a dig in the ribs from Evelyn.

"Pax."

"What? I waited. I just want to know if she's getting the goods."

"Pax!" Evelyn and Callie called.

"Fine," she grumbled.

Taamira thought for a moment; she desperately needed some advice from people who knew of such things better than she did then took the plunge.

"We are more than friends, but we haven't... I mean, we haven't..."

"Had sex," Callie stated gently.

"Yes... I mean no, we have not done that yet."

Pax inclined her head. "But you've done other things?"

"We have kissed and touched over clothes but nothing more." Taamira touched a hand to her face as her cheeks burned with the admission.

"Do you want more than that?" Evelyn asked as she leaned back and stuck her fork in her cheesecake.

Taamira set her full plate on the coffee table and clasped her fingers. "I do. I want more, but I am also scared."

Pax leaned forward and took her hand. "Scared of what, honey? Liam would never hurt you or force you to do anything."

Taamira smiled and squeezed Pax's hand. "I know this, and I am not scared of him hurting me, but that I will disappoint him. I am much less knowledgeable about this than he is."

Evelyn leaned forward and placed her empty plate next to Taamira's full one. "Can I ask a personal question?"

Taamira nodded.

"Are you a virgin?"

Taamira nodded. "Yes, it is the tradition of my culture not to have relations before marriage."

"And is marriage what you want from Liam?"

Taamira shook her head. "I do not know. I care for him very deeply, and when I am with him, nothing else seems to matter, not my country, my traditions, or my family. He makes me feel..." Taamira searched for the words.

"Like you're the centre of everything," Callie stated.

Taamira looked at her with excitement. "Yes. As if I am special."

"You are special, sweetie," Pax said.

"I am not worthy of a man like him. He thinks it is the other way around, but he is so worldly and brave, and I am a fake."

"No, you're a warrior in your own way." Evelyn stood abruptly, and Taamira glanced up at her. "You've lived in a place where you never felt accepted or loved and never relaxed for fear of someone sticking the metaphorical knife in your back. Yet, instead of becoming bitter and cold, you want to use your status to help, to educate people, to help the women of your country. Don't tell me you're not worthy because you are, and Liam knows it too."

Tears prick her eyes at the kindness they showed her. "What if he does not wish to wait until marriage?"

"Is that what you want?"

"I don't know. I am trying to figure out if my culture is still a part of me that I want to keep, but I do not know yet. At the moment, Liam is more important than anything, and I want us to share this connection on every level."

"Then Liam will wait, and if he doesn't, then he's not the man I think he is. But trust me, Liam cares for you. Alex told me he's seen it."

"As for your traditions and history, you'll know when the time is right to move things forward with Liam, and if that involves marriage and you want that, he'll wait and if it doesn't involve your cultural traditions and you still want to wait, then that's your choice. Personally, I think you should play it by ear. You'll know when you know."

"How did you know when it was Blake?"

"When he washed my hair after my attack. He was so gentle and tender with me, and he never left my side the whole time."

Taamira turned to Callie. "And you?"

"When he made sure my dog was safe even though everything was going to hell around us."

Taamira glanced at Evelyn.

"The moment I set eyes on him when I was six years old, and

when we were reunited it was the second he showed me the room he'd set up in his home for me to paint in, in case he ever found me."

She sighed with emotion, her hand coming to her heart at that story, as she looked at the women surrounding her—her new friends—and Taamira realised Liam had given her this too and she fell even deeper for him.

CHAPTER SEVENTEEN

LIAM SIGHED as he saw his home come into view. He and Alex had been up since the ass crack of dawn, both wanting to get the early start so they could get home. Liam smiled to himself at the thought of home, which was something he'd not done in a good long while. He and Alex had checked the venue as best they could, and all threats had been mitigated as much as possible.

When they were both happy with how to move forward, they had emailed a plan to Jack for him to approve and left. The only worry that Liam couldn't get out of his head was her brother's attendance, but he had no plans to leave Taamira's side while she was there so that would hopefully eradicate that one.

Grabbing his overnight bag from the boot of his car, he stepped in the front door and heard music coming from the kitchen and the scent of something sweet. He dropped his head in the office and saw Waggs working on his laptop.

Waggs looked up, eyebrow raised. "Get everything sorted?"

"As much as possible. You know how these things go."

Waggs pursed his lips. "That I do, my friend."

Liam jerked his thumb over his shoulder. "The Princess in the kitchen?"

Waggs chuckled. "Well, it ain't Mitch baking and listening to pop music."

"Best go see if I have a kitchen left."

Liam dropped his bag and strode to the kitchen. He entered quietly and leaned his shoulder on the door jamb as he watched Taamira jigging to the music as she overfilled a pie shell with apple. The grin on his face tipped in a full-blown smile as he watched her make herself at home in his kitchen, and a feeling of completeness settled around him.

Liam moved forward quietly and slipped his hands around her waist, causing her to jump and shriek, as she tried to spin.

"Princess, it's just me."

He saw her fright turn into happiness at the sight of him.

"You're home!"

She didn't know how right she was when she said that, and another lock clicked into place around his heart.

"Yeah, treacle, I'm home."

The light in her eyes shone as she held her messy, sticky hands away from his shirt. His arms rested on her hips, her body close to his, driving him wild as her scent and the softness bombarded him.

"This how you greet me, treacle?"

Her head tipped, and he saw she was taking his words wrong as she tried to step back from him, but he held fast to her and shook his head. "Don't do that. Don't back away from me because you're unsure. If you feel something, then talk to me."

She looked away, not meeting his eyes.

"Taamira."

She looked at him with defiance. "How do I greet you then?"

Her words were said with heat that had him wanting to kiss her until she was putty in his hands. He didn't speak. Instead, he leaned in close and kissed her. At first, she was rigid, but only for a second before she melted into the kiss, opening her mouth for his tongue. He mastered her mouth as he laid claim to her, his hands pulling her closer so she would know what she did to him. How much he wanted her, he wanted there to be no doubt as to what he wanted.

He thought he would die from the need to touch her, her blunt fingernails dug into his shoulders as her tits flattened against him, making his dick so hard he thought he would combust from the need to feel her tight heat surrounding him. It was only the remembrance that she was a virgin that had him pulling back.

Liam gazed down into her flushed face, saw the drugged look of desire in her eyes and wondered if he looked the same way. Never had a woman made him want in this way, never had one responded so completely to his touch.

"Now, that was a greeting."

"Is that what you want?"

"If that's how you want to give it, but yes, that would be my preference."

"I think it's a good way to say hello to people." The smirk on her lips showed she was teasing him, but he growled anyway.

"Not people, Princess. Only me."

"As you wish."

Liam looked behind her at the mess and quirked an eyebrow. "What you cooking?"

Taamira sighed. "The girls introduced me to something called Pinterest, and it has these lovely recipes they say are easy, but this is trickier than I thought."

"I'm sure it will be fine. Is that for tonight?"

"Yes, I wanted to surprise you."

Liam's heart warmed with emotion that she wanted to do this for him. It was difficult to believe this was the same woman from twelve months ago.

"Thank you, that means a lot."

Her smile was radiant as she replied, "You are most welcome."

Liam pulled away so that she could continue doing her thing, but he didn't go far, just leaned against the counter. "What did you think of the girls? The picture Blake sent me showed you having fun."

"Oh, I did. They are so nice, and they gave me some very sound advice."

Liam tensed slightly. "They did?"

"Yes, I wanted to talk to you about it later if that is okay?"

"Of course, that sounds great. How about I take a shower, and then you can relax for a few hours while I work to get everything in place for the speech. Can we talk over dinner?"

She nodded. "Yes, that does sound good."

Liam lifted his chin and moved to the door but stopped when she called his name.

"Liam?"

"Yes, Princess?"

"I missed you."

His grin was ear to ear then. "I missed you too, treacle."

Then he moved to get his work done because the only thing he wanted right then was to have her all to himself.

THEY HAD EATEN a dinner of chicken sandwiches followed by Taamira's very first homemade apple pie, which had been delicious and now they were curled up on the lounge. Her head resting on his chest, he relaxed deeper into her, content and happier than he'd ever been just to be in the moment, but he didn't lie to himself that he didn't want more, he knew in his heart he did.

She was the most stunning woman he had ever met, his reaction to her physically had been unquestionable from the very beginning, but he'd locked it away as a fantasy. A fantasy that he'd used for his pleasure on multiple occasions—fuck who was he kidding—hundreds of occasions.

Taamira had indicated that she wanted to talk earlier, but she hadn't said what about or broached the subject again, and he was hesitant to push her, but he was curious what advice the girls had given her.

He rubbed her shoulder, and her dreamy face turned up to his with a smile.

"You said you wanted to talk?"

Taamira scooted to a full sitting position and frowned. "I do."

Liam reached out and smoothed the frown from her brow with his thumb, and her face softened at his touch. "What's on your mind?"

He waited for her to get her words together, his heart hammering with every second as he waited for her to voice what was on her mind. Was this the moment she would figure out he wasn't worth it, that she would kick his ass to the curb? He didn't say a word despite wanting to, knowing whatever she had to say had been given a lot of thought.

"These last few days, since we decided to see how things went with us being more than friends, I have given my upbringing a lot of thought."

Okay, not what he thought she would say.

"When I was growing up, the traditions of my people were important to me. It helped shape me into who I am."

"I respect that."

She smiled. "I know you do, and I appreciate it, but let me finish."

Liam grinned at her reprimand.

"Since my attack I have... I have not been the same. Those conventional ways are what inhibit the women of my country, and when I needed them, those same traditions allowed me to carry the blame for a crime against me."

He let the growl rumble up his throat at her words but stayed silent.

"But after you and I talked, I wanted to decide if my culture and traditions had any bearing on my future. If it was something I still wanted in my life."

Liam felt terrible that he hadn't known she was struggling with this. "Treacle, if this is about us moving forward in a physical sense, then I'm happy to wait. I don't see this as short term. I'm in this for the long haul. However long that maybe."

"Thank you, but it is not necessary to say that. I have decided that whether you and I continue or not, although I want that immensely, I no longer find that my traditional upbringing and culture define me. It is a part of me, and always will be, but it is not me. It was not of my choosing, and I don't believe it represents me or what I believe to be the truth. So, I will no longer consider living my life around those rules but live it by what I want my future to look like."

Liam blinked his shock away, not knowing what to say for a moment, then he recovered his shock. "This is a big decision Taamira. Don't rush into it. Make sure it's what you want and truly believe is right for you. I don't pretend to know everything about your culture, but I do know it's common for people to want to make changes after a traumatic event."

"I have given this thought. I know that is a possibility but do not feel this is the case for me."

"I understand that some of the practices might seem like they don't fit with how you want women to be treated, but from what little I know from serving in the middle east, the practises are not always exact to what the elders believe."

"I know, and I love that you are happy to discuss this, but my decision is final. Now, this way, I can be with you fully."

Realisation dawned, and Liam sat forward, taking her hand. "Taamira, I love that you want to be with me, and God knows I want you so bad I can hardly see straight but don't make me, or us, the reason you walk away from your history. If you do, then make sure it's for you. I'll be here regardless of whether I have to wait until we're married."

Taamira's mouth dropped open at his words. "Married!"

"Well, not now obviously, but how else did you see this ending if we stay together?"

"Well, I don't know. I guess I never thought past the next few weeks."

"Until this minute neither had I, but I've come to realise that I don't just care for you, Princess, I'm in love with you."

"You are?"

"Yes, I am. And if you want to wait for intimacy, then we will."

CHAPTER EIGHTEEN

TAAMIRA SAT at Liam's desk having taken over the space somewhat with her papers. She'd just hung up from a call with Callie regarding her charity. Setting up anything like that was always time-consuming and never as simple as people thought. But Callie had a lot of knowledge and was a quick learner.

It had taken her no time at all to talk Taamira into being a board member of her new charity Solis. As the charity would be focusing on a broad spectrum, a neutral name had been a good call by Callie and Taamira very much looked forward to working with her more in the coming months.

The door behind her opened and she turned, a smile already on her lips as Liam approached her with his own smile.

He stopped behind her chair; his hands tucked in his pockets. "How's it going?" He nodded at the work she had spread out everywhere.

"Good." She nodded. "I just finished up with Callie, and I am going to be on the board as an advisor."

Liam's eyes lit up. "That's great news. She'll really benefit from your experience."

"I hope I can bring something to the table."

He reached out and twirled a curl of her hair around his finger gently. "You always bring something to the table, treacle."

Heat bloomed in her belly as desire flooded her from the way he was looking at her. They had still not taken things further than kissing. She knew it was because he didn't want to push her to do anything she wasn't ready for, but the fact was, she was so ready to belong to this man in every way possible. It went against her current fight for equal rights, but that was how she felt.

"Thank you for saying that."

"My pleasure, Princess."

She saw the desire in his eyes flare as she stood, coming to read this man was more natural and easier with every day. He hid nothing from her, always fought in her corner and valued her in a way she had never been valued before.

His hands moved to her waist, and she loved that he could span her middle with his hands, feeling small and protected.

"Ready to go to dinner?"

They had agreed to go to dinner at Pax and Blake's home tonight. It had been Pax's idea, but Liam had thought it a good one and so had she. She was talking with these women daily now.

One or another of them checked in on her daily and she realised what she had been missing out on all her life. They didn't call to bitch or moan about the other, they called to say hi, or fill her in on something they deemed relevant in some way. They seemed to care about her, and by extension, they had become necessary to her.

She could not lie to herself though, being with Liam in his home away from the world around them was her favoured place to be. In under a week, this place had become home to her. Life had smoothed out and become what she had always wanted it to be.

"Yes. Have I got time to change?"

He looked her over from head to foot, and she fought the desire to squirm under his intensity. "You can, but just to say, you look perfect as you are."

"Really?" Taamira looked down at the dark blue jeans she was wearing with a cream floaty blouse, flat burgundy ballet pumps on her feet.

"Really." He pulled her closer as he spoke, bending so his words feathered his breath on her neck.

She shivered and leaned in closer to his hard body. Liam had a way of working her up so that her entire body tingled with a need she couldn't quite define.

"I want you in my bed tonight."

Taamira drew in a shaky breath at his words, just the tone he used sent her pulse hammering. His lips skimmed her neck, and she arched against him to give him better access to her body. The growl in his throat had power flowing through her as his lips landed on hers, and he kissed her with a demanding passion she hadn't known from him before.

It showed a wilder uninhibited side to him she hadn't yet seen, but she liked it. In fact, she loved it. Her fingers wove through his hair, scraping his scalp with her short nails and eliciting a groan from him before he pulled back, dropping several shorter kisses on her lips as he did.

His eyes were dark and hooded with desire and love for her. She still could not believe he had said those words to her, but it was difficult to doubt them when he showed her every day how much he cared. Taamira had not said them back, wanting to choose a moment they would remember for her to tell him she loved him too.

"You good with sharing my bed? I won't expect a single fucking thing from you, but I'm done waking up without you."

"Can we do some stuff and see how that goes?" she asked, a flutter of nerves hammering at her neck at the excitement the thought of being with this handsome man elicited.

"We can do whatever you want, Princess. You're in charge."

Just like that, her nerves were gone and even though she was the novice, the virgin, a heady power surged through her because he gave her that.

Taamira nodded and then went to freshen her make-up, deciding to leave her clothes as they were. If Liam liked what she wore, then that was good enough for her. Plus, Pax had said it was casual.

As THEY PULLED into the drive of the house Pax and Blake shared, Taamira let a smile tilt her lips. The home was new, as were all the others on the development, but they weren't on top of each other. Each was detached with its own garage, front garden, and from what Liam said, a sizeable back garden too.

Liam came to her side of the car and opened the door for her. It was easy to forget the threat hanging over her most of the time as he didn't bring it up. In his home they were cocooned in safety but watching the way he looked around before her ushering her quickly to the door where Pax was standing waiting for them with Blake, reminded her that life was not as perfect as she had been pretending.

"Come in, come in. Let me take your coats," Pax said as she shoved the coats at Blake who rolled his eyes playfully.

Pax took her arm and guided her towards the living room, which was beautiful and airy but inviting and cosy at the same time. It was classic and timeless, just like the woman who lived there.

Taamira heard Liam behind her talking with Blake, but she concentrated on her new friend as she glanced around the beautiful home.

"Do you want the tour?"

Taamira nodded. "Yes, please."

She wanted to see the place her friend called home, and as she admired each new room, she loved it more, seeing little touches she would like to add to Liam's home if they got to that stage and he would allow it. He had taken great pains to renovate his farmhouse, and she loved it, but it did lack a certain softness.

As they ended up back in the kitchen that led to an open plan dining room where a large table was laid with silver wear and candles, she found Liam and Blake easily chatting.

"Did you see the cushions?" Blake asked as he tipped a beer to his lips.

Taamira frowned, unsure what he meant.

"Ignore him," Pax said with an eyeroll at her man. "He doesn't understand that cushions on a bed are an aesthetic."

"They're a pain in my ass is what they are, woman," he said as he reached out and pulled her to his side, looking at her with a grin before dropping a kiss on her lips.

The look of love between these two made her feel like she was intruding until Liam pulled her back to his front, resting his chin on her shoulder, his arms around her waist, warm against her body.

Pax cast a look their way and grinned before turning to Blake. "Anything I can do?"

"Nah, babe, you go relax. I just need to give the tempura batter another whisk." He winked at Pax who looked at Taamira.

"Did you ever think that sentence would sound so sexy?"

Taamira laughed but liked seeing this different side of Blake.

Pax wandered over to the side unit, which held a vast array of bottles of varying varieties.

Pax picked up a blue bottle of liquid, giving it a shake. "Do you like blueberries, Taamira?"

"Yes, very much."

"Then you're going to love this Blueberry Mojito mocktail."

Pax set about mixing the drink for her after she handed Liam a beer. Pax didn't skimp on presentation, sugaring the edge of the glass for effect. She handed it to Taamira, her hands clasped together in glee as Taamira took a sip and the fresh, minty, fruit flavour burst on her tongue.

"Ohh, that is delicious."

She saw Liam wince and Blake chuckled as he did and she wondered what she had done to cause that response, but then Blake announced dinner was ready.

They took their places at the table as he served them a delightful starter of tempura vegetables, followed by seabass with a citrus salsa, green beans, and parmesan potatoes.

"So, how do you like Hereford?" Blake asked.

"I haven't seen a lot of it yet, but what I have, I like very much."

"Great place to bring up a family," Pax said with a grin and wink at her.

Taamira dropped her eyes at the blatant attempt to find out more about her and Liam.

"Gracie, leave them alone."

Taamira looked up, not having heard Blake call her that before and saw the soft look Pax gave him.

Liam reached over and took her hand in his, rubbing his thumb over her knuckles as he gave her the same soft look Pax gave Blake. "I plan on showing Taamira around when I get two minutes."

Pax leaned into Blake as their hands stayed linked together and Taamira found it strange but beautiful. In her culture it was not done to show affection, in fact, she could not remember her brother ever looking at his wife that way.

A vague memory of her father and mother surfaced, and she wondered if it was a memory or a dream. It was incredibly sad to her that love was so often viewed as a weakness. She had never seen such strength shared between two people and she knew if she and Liam continued in this vein, they would become that same solid, unbreakable unit.

They continued to chat as they ate dessert, which was strawberry custard tarts Pax had made, in the living room with coffee. She loved hearing the stories Blake shared about his time as a guard for the Queen and her daughter.

Having met and liked them, Taamira found it familiar territory which she had worried about before they arrived. Fitting in with these people was important to her because they were important to Liam.

As the night wore on and the couples relaxed, she found herself curled into Liam's arm on the couch as Pax took a similar position tucked into Blake. Around ten she tried to stifle a yawn and Liam looked down at her.

"Time to get you home to bed."

His words were innocuous, but the promise in them caused a little shiver as she thought of what was to come. The night had been perfect, and she hoped it would end with her being fully Liam's and him being hers.

CHAPTER NINETEEN

As he closed and locked the door to his home, securing them for the night, Liam took a long breath. He needed to control the desire that burned through his blood every time he thought of the woman who was looking at him with wonder, excitement, and a touch of fear. It was that fear that gave him the strength to settle his desire. The last few days had been like a dream come true; a dream Liam hadn't even known he wanted and yet here he was living a life that made him happier than he ever had been.

Whatever happened between them tonight would be entirely up to her. He knew what his body wanted—his dick was all for the stupendous release he knew he would have when he got inside her body. His head, however, wanted this to be about her. It was arrogant, but he knew he could make her feel things she'd never dreamed of. The connection they shared was like nothing he'd ever had before.

Sauntering towards her, he loved how her back straightened, and she looked up at him with an unbending spirit. It was that spirit he'd first fallen in love with he realised now. Her beauty was unparallel in his eyes, but it was her fierce will to overcome anything put in her way, the kind gentleness she showed to others that had him falling hopelessly in love with her.

Lifting his hand, he brushed her cheek with his fingers as he tucked a piece of hair behind her ear. "You're in charge here, Taamira. Nothing happens that you don't want. I need you to know that. If it means we wait, then we wait until you're ready."

Her fingers moved to cover his lips. "I'm ready, honey."

His heart leapt at the small endearment that meant so much. No one had ever used one on him before and he found he liked it, a lot.

With no further words, he took her hand and walked up the stairs to his bedroom. He looked at it through her eyes, noting the masculine colours. He'd make sure to tell her she could redecorate, do whatever she needed to do to make this her home as much as it was his. Of course, they hadn't actually had a conversation about the future, he'd steamrolled over her a little with that, but he just didn't see a future where she wasn't front and centre for him.

Moving to the bed, he sat and pulled her between his legs. Looking up at her as she gazed trustingly down at him with all her emotions evident on her face, he waited with his heart in his throat until she bent to him, pressing her lips to his. He let her lead; her kiss less innocent than before but still had a sweetness about it that turned him on.

He growled in his throat when she touched her tongue to his lips and pulled her onto his lap, taking over. He held himself in check as he kissed her slowly, languidly until she was pliant in his arms, almost melting into his body, her arms around his neck, her fingertips playing with his hair.

Liam relaxed back onto the bed until she was lying half over him, her body pressed over his in a perfect fit. Raising his hand, he drifted it over her hair, following the curve of her body over her shoulder to her hip and inched his hand under her blouse. Her skin was like the purest silk, soft and perfect to his rough hands. She shivered and he knew it was with desire as she pressed her body closer wanting more.

Skirting his finger under the lace edge of her bra, he pulled the cup down, releasing her perfect tits to his touch. The nipple beaded, and he fought the need to race this, he wanted her first experience of everything to be perfect. Her tits filled his palm, and his dick strained against his jeans, desperate to slide into her tight wetness.

Pulling away, he looked into her clouded with passion eyes, her lips swollen from his kiss and knew he'd remember this night for the rest of his life. As he kept his focus on her, he began to unbutton her top, revealing her silky, warm skin to him. Her tits were a vision, high and proud, the nipples a dark brown and begging for his mouth on them.

Leaning in, he took a perky nipple in his mouth and twirled his tongue around it before sucking lightly. Her back arched, and she held his head where she wanted him, her natural sensuality leading her. He bit down on the tender nub and as she moaned his name, his dick jumped.

He administered the same treatment to the other nipple before blowing lightly on the wet skin and smiling at her shiver. He knew this slow build-up would make it better for her, and although he prayed to every god he could name that she didn't, it also gave her the time to change her mind if that was what she wanted.

Taamira shed her blouse and unhooked her bra in a bold move that had him growling in his throat. Her confidence, even in this, was a turn on to him.

"So fucking beautiful." He brushed his fingers over her waist, her timid fingers resting at the edge of his shirt, tickling his skin. "Touch me, beautiful. I want to feel your hands on me."

Her delicate touches were like the sweetest torture as she trailed her fingertips over his belly as his muscles tensed. He allowed her to explore his abdomen and chest before he sat up and drew his shirt over his head, tossing it to the floor without care.

Lying back, he pulled her so she was straddling him, putting her firmly in the driver's seat. She took the cue and leaned over to kiss him, but he wanted her gorgeous tits in his face. As she moved, he latched his mouth to her nipple and drew it deep, loving the feel of her on his skin.

"Oh," she murmured.

He held her in place with his hand in the middle of her back as he feasted on her. She rubbed her centre against his aching cock, and he groaned against her skin.

"Liam," she chanted.

He knew she was overwhelmed by the desire racing through her and didn't know what to do with it. He released her, and his mouth met hers in a hot kiss that was building in passion with every swipe of their tongues.

Pulling away, he stood then knelt on the floor, putting his hand in the middle of her chest as he gently pushed her to her back on the bed. She propped herself up on her elbows, her natural curiosity winning out as he began to unbutton the jeans she wore.

"Lift up."

She complied, eagerly lifting her ass so he could draw her jeans down her spectacular legs and toss them aside. Her white lace knickers were sexy as hell but what was sexier was the wetness he could see there. Her evident desire for him made him want to roar like some sort of Viking conqueror.

Pulling her knickers down her legs, he tossed them aside and gazed at her slick pussy. A thin strip of dark hair running up the middle had his mouth-watering, he wanted to taste every last drop of her desire.

Hands on the inside of her knees, he pushed her legs apart, wedging his shoulders between them. Her hand moved to her tits to cover them in a sudden flare of shyness and Liam stayed her hand.

"Don't hide this perfection from me, treacle." He released her, and she let her hand drop, but he could see the pulse in her neck beating and needed to know it was from desire, not fear. "You good?"

She nodded hastily, and he grinned. "Give me the words, beautiful."

"I want you, Liam. I want to feel it all with you. Make me yours."

Her words lit a fire that ripped through him, and he bent his head, nipping and kissing his way up her thighs on either side before he finally put them out of their misery and put his mouth where they both needed it.

He licked her from the edge of her opening to the hood of her clit, flicking the sensitive nub with his tongue. She writhed beneath him, her breath coming in short gasps as her climax hovered. Knowing she was nice and wet, he circled her pussy with his finger and she tensed slightly with nerves.

"Relax, treacle. I won't hurt you."

Instantly she relaxed, and he entered her the tiniest bit, the tight, wet, heat hugging his finger as he moved it slowly inside her, all the time using his tongue to keep her on the edge of her climax but not falling over.

He added a second finger, and she didn't flinch, too lost in the moment to notice as he worked her body. She was putty in his hands and yet she had never had so much control over him. In that second, she owned him completely. Crooking his finger, he rubbed the sensitive spot inside her and bit down gently on her clit, and she ignited.

Her body arched off the bed as her climax shook through her, the sweet taste of her flooded his mouth and he lapped up every drop of her release. She screamed his name over and over, her body shaking, her pussy squeezing his fingers with the power of it, as it crested and then rolled through her, coming in smaller aftershocks until she was boneless beneath him.

Giving her body one more lick, her legs squeezing him as she shuddered, he climbed up her body and smiled down at her, the look on her face pure emotion before he kissed her.

Her hands gripped his back as she kissed him back, seeming to enjoy the taste of herself on him, which he found extremely erotic.

"That was...." She stopped seeming to not have the words.

"That was a warmup," he teased as he stood and put his hand to his fly. "You sure you want this?" he asked before he released his zipper.

He may very well die if she said she wasn't ready, but he would prefer that to her doing something she wasn't ready for.

"I want this, more than I have ever wanted anything. I just don't want to disappoint you."

Liam stilled his hand, ignoring his angry dick. "Taamira, there is nothing you can do on this Earth that would disappoint me. What we just shared was better than anything I've ever had before. Seeing you here, now, laid out before me like a fucking goddess makes me feel like a king, and if all I get to do is look at you like that, then I'll die a privileged and happy man."

Her features went soft at his words, and she sat up, her hands going to his zipper and pushing his fingers out of the way. "No dying," she admonished him. "I want to do lots of things with you, starting with you making love to me."

Her fingers lowered the zip, and his dick screamed in relief at having more room. Going commando now seemed like a bad idea as Taamira pulled in a sharp breath. He looked down as Taamira caressed his cock with her wide eyes.

"Will it fit?"

Liam let the chuckle move through him as he tilted her head, so she was looking at his face instead. "It'll fit, Princess. Do you want to know why?"

Taamira angled her head to look at him. "Why?"

"Because you were born for me and I for you." It sounded cheesy in his head but spoken it sounded worse, and he winced. He needn't have; her expression told him it was just what she needed to hear.

Her hand came to his cock, and she tentatively gripped his length as he gritted his teeth, pleasure ripping through his body. Liam held his hand over hers, gripping harder and she glanced at him in surprise as he showed her how to work his cock.

"It won't break, Taamira."

He released his hand and she continued her exploration of his dick, working him, her light fingers cupping his ball sack as he groaned in pleasure. Taamira instantly released him her eyes shooting to his in question.

"So good, beautiful," he said as he took her hand and put it back on his cock.

He watched her part her lips, touching her tongue to the soft sensitive skin on the underside of his cock. He couldn't wait for her to put those lips around his cock, but that was not for today. Today was about her, teaching her what she liked and how to open herself to the pleasure he could give her. With that thought he pulled away from her grasp, smiling at the little moan of displeasure she gave before he reached for a condom in his bedside draw and her eager eyes lit up.

Never had rolling a condom down his length been such a sensual experience but with her watching his every move, innocent desire in her eyes, it most definitely was. To the point that if he didn't get himself in check, he'd blow his load like a teenage boy.

Leaning over her, he settled her back on the bed and nestled himself between her legs, her warm wetness caressing the tip of his cock was heaven. Liam linked his fingers through hers, bringing them up above her head, so her perky tits brushed his chest. "Thank you for giving me this gift, Taamira. I will treasure this until the day I die."

Her eyes filled with liquid warmth. "I love you, Liam Hayes."

"I know you do, treacle," he said with a smirk before he kissed her and pushed into her slowly.

Her body took him, a tiny bit of resistance to begin with, her virgin body so tight it hugged him like a vice. He kissed her through it, the passion building as her pussy became wet with her pleasure. He stopped for a second once he was fully inside her, pulling back to look at her, needing to know she was okay. The thought of hurting her in any way had him sick to his stomach.

"Did I hurt you?"

Taamira shook her head, then wiggled her hips. "No, but I need you to move."

"Have I told you how perfect you are?"

He grinned and then began to move. Her tits bounced with every thrust as he watched the skin on her body flush with her building climax.

Taamira wrapped her legs around his back, and he moaned her name as he went deeper, his movements becoming faster and faster, prickles of electricity building in his balls, his pelvis rubbing her clit with every inward stroke.

He'd never experienced anything like this, it was more than physical, it was visceral, a connection only they shared as their eyes stayed connected.

"Liam." Her voice sounded panicked and desperate as her release barrelled down on her with so much intensity he could see it frightened her.

"It's okay, Princess. I have you. Just let go and I'll catch you, I'll always catch you."

At his words, her pussy pulsed around him as she cried out his name, chanting it like a prayer. He watched her with awe as he continued to fuck her, no make love to her, before he allowed his own release to take him, pulling him to a place he had never been before, showing him what he had been missing his whole life—her. He'd not known joy until she came into his life. As he looked at her satisfied smile, Liam knew he would die before he ever let anyone take her away from him. The thought terrified him because to love that much made him vulnerable to a pain so staggering he knew he wouldn't survive if it were lost.

CHAPTER TWENTY

THE SWITCH in Liam from devoted boyfriend to deadly bodyguard was slightly jarring. It wasn't anything he had done per se, but more his demeanour. He was still close to her, not leaving her side, but the little touches and the intimate grins had ceased. She knew why; he was worried about her being out in the open with the threat still looming and was concentrating on her safety. Understanding didn't stop her missing it and yearning for things to go back to how they were.

They were drawing up to the hotel with a full complement of guards. In the past she would have thought it was overkill but having been on the receiving end of multiple threats, she was more than happy to concede to the experts on this. Taamira was stubborn; she was not, however, stupid.

She had been delighted to see some of the men from Fortis when she arrived at the airfield with Liam, Jack, Alex, Mitch, and Lopez. Zack, the leader of Fortis, had greeted her with warmth, as had the other men.

Liam had relaxed on the flight, even coming to sit with her for a while until she had fallen asleep. Her nights had become a lot more active than they ever had, with Liam waking her in differing and inventive ways that had her body singing to his tune.

She smiled at the memory of this morning as she sat in the car beside him, Alex and Mitch in the front. Zack was driving the car behind them, with Dane, K, and Zin. In the lead car were Jack and Lopez.

"When we get to the hotel, we wait until Jack and Lopez have cleared the lobby before we get you inside," Liam said for the second time.

Taamira laid a hand on his arm. "I know, honey," she reassured.

The convoy of cars stopped and the men, all wearing earpieces and wrist comms exited, smart jackets and trousers covering the watches they all wore to communicate. Liam bounced his leg in a rare show of tension as they waited the few moments it took to clear the entrance of any apparent threats.

Jack came back and opened her door as Liam exited on his own side and moved around to her side, his body close as he could be, his arm protectively around her. He ushered her through the door to the hotel where they would stay, and the conference would take place.

Taamira barely had a second to appreciate the exquisite décor in the lobby before they ushered her into the lift. Another man went to step in, and Jack stepped in front of her as Liam acted as her shield. "Get the next one, buddy."

The older man blustered for a second but then the doors closed on him. Inside the lift, Jack turned to Liam. "Zack and his team are clearing the floor."

Liam gave a short nod but remained quiet. Taamira could not help but think more was going on than she knew. It was her own fault; she was not ignorant of her personal safety, but she was perhaps a little oblivious. She trusted these men; they knew what they were doing, and she never questioned that. "Is everything alright?"

Liam frowned and looked to Jack who gave the smallest of shrugs.

She turned to look at Liam a question in her eyes. "Liam?"

"Your brother is here."

The words cut through her like a knife, pain hitting her in the middle of her chest at the proclamation. It should not hurt her as it did, but the loss of her brother still stung after all this time. "How do you know?"

"Lopez picked him up on the cameras earlier today. We tried to change the booking, but all the hotels in the area were booked with delegates."

The elevator stopped, and Jack put himself in front of the door, his head tilted, and she knew from experience he was getting an update from someone. "Clear."

The doors opened at his word, and they rushed her towards the open door of her suite. Zack and K were covering one end of the empty hall and its entrance, and Zin and Dane were covering the other, their intent focused on any threat that was foolish enough to attempt access.

Once inside the suite, with the door closed, she moved to the low leather couch, dropping her handbag, and kicking off her heels. It was amazing and freeing to her that in the last few weeks she had become so relaxed in the presence of these men that she thought nothing of kicking off her shoes and relaxing her mask of Princess. Perhaps it was because these men were not just her guards now; they were friends of the man she had given her heart to.

Lopez was walking around the room with a wand of sorts as Jack and Liam set up computers on a nearby table.

"I want both rooms on either side of us occupied by the team and a wire in the Prince's room. If he sneezes, I want to know about it."

"Is that necessary?" Taamira asked as she went to him, leaning a hand on his bent back, in what was now a familiar move. The thought of someone spying on her brother made her uneasy.

Liam straightened and turned to her, his face hard, brooking no argument. "Yes, it is."

"Could we not just monitor who goes in and out and leave him his privacy? The thought of that invasion does not sit well with me."

Liam cupped her cheek, eyes soft as he looked at her with all of the love he had for her. "How can you still show him such compassion? After everything they have done, you still care."

"It is not easy to turn off feelings many years in the growing, and I cannot erase the history we share. A history that was happy for the most part and even when we became less close, Abdul always showed me kindness, at least until the attack." Her voice shook slightly on the last word, and Liam reached for her hand.

He seemed to give it some thought before he nodded and turned to Lopez. "Wire the halls, nobody goes in or out that we don't know about."

"Thank you, Liam." She placed a kiss on his cheek.

He grinned. "Anything for you, treacle."

"You sure about this, Liam?" Jack asked as he stood next to the computers, his hands on his hips, waiting.

Liam nodded. "Yes, it's what she wants."

Taamira could see Jack disagreed, and it was on the tip of her tongue to ask him why when the phone in the suite rang.

Liam looked at Jack. "Anyone know we're in this suite?"

"Only our team and they have direct lines to us all. Nobody should know which room we're in." Jack walked to the phone and picked it up. "Yes," he said curtly and Taamira watched as he listened, everyone silent until he shook his head. "You're a major pain in my ass, Astrid."

Tension leaked from the room, and everyone went about what they were doing, but Taamira continued to watch Jack until he hung up quickly. "Is everything okay?"

Jack looked at her, his face wearing an irritated expression that she had not seen on him before. "Yeah, Astrid is Zenobi and a huge pain in the ass. She called to prove she could get through our security."

Lopez laughed. "She likes winding Jack up because she wants his trouser snake."

Jack glared at Lopez. "Watch your mouth, Lopez."

Lopez just laughed harder, but he did shut up. Jack and Liam then set about helping Lopez set up the computers to show the hall-ways, and the rooms either side.

"Mitch setting up the platform?" Liam asked.

Jack inclined his head from where he was typing furiously on the laptop. "He's finding a spot for tomorrow night so he can give us overwatch."

"This all seems a lot?" Taamira said as more of a question than a statement.

Liam moved towards her and dropped to his haunches, resting his hand on her knee. She ignored the shiver of awareness his touch gave her.

"It is a lot, but with your brother here, and knowing the last threat came from the Palace, we can't take any chances."

"I understand." And she did, it was just a lot, almost too much for one person. Taamira kissed Liam lightly and stood. "I think I will go over my speech again."

Liam smirked. "That speech is perfect. You've practised it a thousand times."

"I know, but it is missing something essential."

"Okay, treacle."

Liam's watch buzzed then, and at the same time, Jack's phone rang. The two men looked at each other, then Lopez.

"It's an amber alert from Mitch," Lopez said looking at his watch as Jack answered the call, putting it on speakerphone so the other two men could hear.

Her heart leapt to her throat as she waited again, hating this constant state of low-level anxiety she found herself in.

"Talk to me, Mitch."

"Just caught Scott Porter hanging around the service entrance to the kitchen. Where do you want me to take him?"

Taamira drew in a breath as she recognised the name of one of her original guards. Was he the one who had taken the picture of her working out? He had seemed the friendliest of the men, and that was sad. It seemed her instincts about people had let her down again.

"Take him to the guardhouse on the grounds. I'll be there in a few minutes." Jack hit end on the call and immediately called someone else. "Zack, it's me. I need you and Zin to meet Mitch at the guard-house at the back of the hotel. He has one of Princess Taamira's old guards there. Caught the fucker sneaking around."

She did not hear the rest but guessed Zack agreed.

"I'm coming with you," Liam said.

Jack nodded and turned to Lopez. "Do not leave this room. Nobody goes in or out unless it's one of us."

Liam moved towards her, the banging of her heart in her chest the only sign of fear. She did not want him to leave. She liked and trusted Lopez, but nobody made her feel safe like Liam did. Inter-nally she pulled herself together and took a calming breath.

"I need to question him. Will you be okay with Lopez? I can stay if you prefer."

That was her Liam, always putting her first. "No, go. I will be fine here with Lopez."

"Are you sure?" He looked concerned his brows drawn into a frown.

"Go, find out what Scott is up to so that we can put this behind us."

He nodded and leaned in to take her mouth in a kiss that had her toes curling as she leaned in close before he pulled away with a grin. "Later."

The growled word had every erogenous zone she knew of sitting up.

She walked with him to the door and stepped back as he and Jack left, bereft at the loss of him already and knowing it was silly, but she had never had a connection like it before and knew she never would again. Perhaps it was something she could ask Pax or Callie about, speaking to Evelyn about absence was crazy stupid after the prolonged time apart she and Alex had endured.

"I'm going to take a shower, Manny." She called Lopez by his

Christian name, not liking the way everyone called him by his surname.

"Sure thing, Princess T."

Taamira shook her head at his nickname for her and grinned as she went to the bedroom suite and closed the door.

As she moved about the room, collecting things for her shower, and unpacking the bags that were delivered earlier, she opened her vanity case and stopped dead. An envelope with her brother's familiar looped handwriting sat on top of her make-up. A curl of insecurity moved over her, and she found herself looking around for some sign of the person who had put it there. It was not her brother but if not him, then who and why?

Sitting heavily on the bed she reached for the envelope, ripping it open and unfolding the single sheet of thick, cream paper with the headed crest of her family in the centre in gold print.

TAAMIRA,

Meet me at the hotel restaurant at 3:30 pm. I need to talk with you and clear up this misunderstanding. Our estrangement has gone on for too long, and it is time to end this nonsense.

Abdul.

SHE GLANCED at the clock on the nightstand and saw it was already 3:25 pm. That did not give her much time to think through her response. In her heart, she knew this was probably a bad idea but the small part of her that remembered her brother reading her a favourite story as a child even though it had been girlie, wanted to go. To give him the chance to say he was wrong, that he regretted what he had done and allowed her to tell him how much he had hurt her.

Mind made up, she considered calling Liam, but he would stop her or at least try. If she told Lopez and the other two men to take her to the restaurant, they would do it.

She knew it would damage the fragile bond she had built with them by behaving in such a way, but she did not have time to worry about that. This would give her the chance to find out if her nieces were safe too.

Standing, she smoothed her skirt and bit back the regret of what she could lose with this move and walked from the room her head held high. It was time to become the high-handed Princess that most people thought she was.

CHAPTER TWENTY-ONE

TAAMIRA KEPT her head high as she walked into the sleek continental restaurant on the first floor of the hotel. To say her directive to Lopez, Dane, and Kanan had not gone well would be an understatement. Initially, Lopez had flatly refused her request until she told him if he did not escort her, she would go on her own.

His look of disappointment had flooded her throat with unshed tears which she had battled to tamp down. She had to keep up this entitled role to get what she needed, perhaps that indeed meant she was entitled.

Dane had immediately called his boss, but fortunately for her, he hadn't picked up, and neither had Jack or Liam when Lopez called them. Thinking of Liam had her step faltering and questioning her plan. He would be so angry she was going against what he had asked of her, but she didn't think she had a choice, plus she had three highly trained men with her. It wasn't like she was slipping away like an idiot to get herself killed.

These men had kept her safe in the past before they even knew her. Dane and Kanan had been the ones to initiate the rescue that had freed her and the rest of the hostages, including their friends, from the gunmen back in St Kitts. She was safer with these men than she had ever been in her life.

After a concise discussion that involved them shooting her several annoyed glances, they had agreed to take her to the restaurant. She had said nothing about the letter knowing that regardless of who she was and what she demanded, they would not agree if they had even the slightest inclination of a threat. The guilt about ambushing them had her tummy aching with anxiety.

With Kanan at her back, Lopez to her left, and Dane to her right, she entered the restaurant and was immediately offered a seat by the window, which she went to accept when Dane had interrupted her.

"We want the table closest to the fire exit facing the entrance."

Taamira deferred to him and followed the concierge towards the table, discreetly looking around the room. She noted politicians, heads of state, and even a duke or two. This hotel was at capacity for high-value targets as she'd heard Liam refer to them, and as such, the amount of security was ridiculous.

Taamira sat and pretended to look at the menu as the men guarding her stood a discreet distance from her on full alert, the tension radiating from their bodies. She knew when they got hold of Liam he would arrive and drag her out of there having no care to who she was, because to him she was just treacle and that was how she liked it. It was how she wanted these men to see her too. She had been on the way to becoming accepted by them, but she'd self-sabotaged that today. She just hoped it was worth it.

Taamira knew the second her brother entered the room, Lopez swore and glanced at her as Dane and Kanan closed the gap instantly shielding her from sight. Kanan lifted his watch and pressed a button before dropping his hand to his side. She didn't know what he'd done, but she figured she didn't have a lot of time.

Taamira stood as she saw her brother and his personal guard stride towards her.

"Did you know about this?" Lopez demanded, turning to her with accusation in his eyes.

"I'm sorry," was her only response and she was sorry.

"God damn it, T."

She did not have the chance to say more though because her brother was there in front of them.

"Move aside for his Royal Highness, The Crown Prince Abdul al Kamali."

Taamira almost rolled her eyes as Mustafa, her brother's head of security announced her brother using his full title. She wanted to tell him none of that held any sway with these men, but she bit her tongue, instead reaching out and laying a hand of Kanan's shoulder. "It's okay, let him through."

Kanan tensed, and she wondered if he was going to ignore her, but with a slight chin lift to Dane, they stepped aside, leaving just enough room for her to move forward, seeing her brother in person for the first time since she had left his boat for the island of St Kitts.

He looked good, regal as he always had but she noticed the imperious manner in which he looked at her men, her friends, if they would still allow it.

"Your men are untrained and uncouth, sister," her brother said in greeting.

Taamira clenched her jaw to stop herself from lashing out at him. She did not have time for a verbal sparring match about these men but oh, how she wanted too. "Brother, you look well."

He eyed her all over critically, and she waited for the blow, but it never came.

"As do you, sister. Are you ready to forget this sulk you have been throwing and come home?"

Taamira was struck speechless by his words, the insensitivity, and the callous way he dismissed her feelings. "Sulk?" she ground out as Lopez moved closer to her back.

Her brother's eyes flicked behind her, and she saw the way he rocked back just the tiniest bit on his heels at what he saw. "I did not mean it to be insulting, but the family needs you. Your nieces miss you. They speak of you often. It is not seemly for an unmarried woman to be galivanting around the world on her own."

Him using her nieces had her temper flaring, but it gave the perfect opportunity to ask about them. "Are they well?"

She saw the pride on his face, and her chest ached, this was the brother she remembered, this was the man she knew, not the one who had sold her out.

"Najwa is studying the arts and Mamina has a fine musical talent."

"And Fawzaana?"

Her brother's wife was not her favourite person in the world; Taamira found her calculating. She had been sweetness and light until they married and once her place as the future Queen was secured she had changed, looking down on people, being harsh and cruel with the staff at the palace, always critical of her daughters, yet she had been nice enough with her, and her brother seemed happy. Although she did not think it was a love match, she saw none of what she and Liam shared between her brother and his wife.

"Fawzaana is well. She is in our rooms resting, the flight tired her."

"Are they safe?"

Her brother frowned. "Of course, they are safe. What happened to you was not ignored, my sister. We have taken every precaution to keep it from happening again. If only you had listened to me, it would not have happened."

Taamira's instant anger flared, but then she let it go. Her brother was not being cruel on purpose; it was just how he saw things. Women should do as instructed, and she had scorned that, and it had ended badly for her. "Why did you not pay the ransom for me? Why was it so easy for you to leave me to the whims of evil men? I understand I went against your word, and that is unforgivable in your world, but I am still your sister, still your Tami."

The pain in her words must have hit her brother, and she saw him accept the verbal blow, but she did not understand the look of confusion on his face.

"Oh, shit," were the hushed words behind her and Taamira lifted her head to see what might have caused those words and saw Liam and Jack bearing down on the group.

Liam's face was like thunder, and Jack didn't seem much happier. Liam moved to her side as Dane and Kanan stepped aside to give him room. He took her arm in a firm but gentle grip, and ignoring the other men, looked at her.

Taamira glanced at his angry face and instantly wanted to soothe him.

"Which part of stay in the room, didn't you understand?"

Taamira bristled but held her tongue, just gave him a look that could freeze lava. The twitch on his lips was the only sign he found her anger amusing.

"Who is this man laying his hands on you in this manner?" her brother demanded.

Taamira and Liam both turned to her brother, who was watching them intently. Especially the familiar way Liam held her. Now was her chance to announce to her family who this man was and what he meant to her. "Abdul, this is Liam Hayes, my boyfriend."

The surprise rippled around the room like a wave, and she glanced at Liam to see his reaction. His eyes had softened, gone warm with love for her, and she wanted to kiss him more than she wished to breathe at that moment, but she held back, not wanting an audience.

"Boyfriend! He is a commoner, a lowly guard. He is not fit to be your anything, Taamira."

She moved to defend Liam but he beat her to it. "You're right, I'm not fit to lick her shoes, yet she loves me, and I love her. There is nothing, and I do mean nothing, I wouldn't do for her, and there's not a single thing in all of your imagination that I wouldn't do to keep her safe from harm."

Taamira's heart gave a jump at his words, and she leaned her body into his as his arm came around her waist. Instantly her world settled at his touch.

Her brother followed the movement, and she saw a sadness in his eyes before they turned hard. "This will end badly. Love is a myth fed to ignorant people to keep them prisoner."

"Love is the only thing that matters, brother. It saddens me that you do not see that, that you do not value the right things. I have love, I have friendship, and I have worth, and that is what matters to me."

The sound of loud clapping from a single person had everyone turning to the sound.

Taamira's legs went weak as the men around her went still. "Father?"

King Saud al Kamali of Eyan was standing just feet away, and he was clapping. "Bravo, my daughter, wise words indeed." He turned to Abdul. "Leave us." His tone was harsh with the authority born from never having his words questioned.

Abdul paused, and she almost wanted him to speak out, to not to be the man he had become, to be the Prince who was strong and questioned people, but his backbone was weak now it seemed. He dipped his head, and he and his guard left without a word.

"Daughter, will you speak with me?"

Taamira straightened her spine, ready to do battle and set this meeting on her terms. "I will speak with you in my suite in twenty minutes."

She watched his look of shock morph into pride. He inclined his head, and she and her entourage swept from the room.

CHAPTER TWENTY-TWO

THE SECOND they walked back into the suite she turned to Liam and the other men, including Dane and Kanan. "I am sorry. I should never have put you in that position. It was wrong of me. I am not that person any longer. I hope you can forgive me?"

The anger she had previously seen on Kanan's and Dane's features left them.

"Princess, you do get that we are both married to stubborn women, right?" Kanan said with a grin that left her in no doubt he adored that stubborn woman and that he forgave her. "Just let Liam keep you safe, all right?"

Taamira nodded, and with tips of their chins, the two Fortis men went to take up their positions in the hallway again.

She turned and looked at Jack and Lopez, not wanting to face Liam just yet. "I hope things can go back to being as they were before. I treated you badly, Manny and I don't want to be that person to you. You are Liam's friend, and I want you to like me."

Lopez chuckled as he moved to her. "I do like you, T. Just don't do that shit again."

Jack just shook his head. "Another pain in my ass." His wink took the heat from his words as he walked away. "I have a bloody King to prepare for now."

Taking a breath, Taamira twisted to Liam who had not left her back the entire time she had been apologising and raised her eyes to his face. Expecting to see annoyance, she found his lips twitching with mirth.

"What is so funny?" She angled her hands up, resting them on his chest as his arms instantly came around her.

"You are."

The smile in his voice relaxed her. "Oh, really?"

"Yeah, really. You just announced to the entire world that the Princess of Eyan is dating some cockney who thinks dark jeans is dressing up and all you're worried about is if my friends like you."

Taamira's heart warmed, her body tilting to him as if drawn by a magnet. "They matter to you, so they matter to me."

"Have you any idea how much guts it took to confront your brother? To tell a King you would speak to him on your terms?"

"It is not seen as brave in my world."

"Well, in mine it is. You are brave, you are caring, and so fucking strong. I'm so proud of you, Taamira. The world needs more women like you."

"Thank you," she said simply because emotion had her eyes wet and her throat constricting.

He didn't stop, though. "Your brother is a fool. He's missing out on so much with his weakness. I see that now. I don't believe he's evil, but he is weak. He will never be half the person you are."

"He was, once."

Liam swiped the tear that had fallen on to her cheek with his thumb before kissing her there lightly. "Maybe he was, and I see the grief in your eyes for the man he was, but that man isn't the one I met today."

"No, he is not."

"I love you, Taamira. I meant every word I said to your brother. I would do anything for you to keep you safe."

"I love you too, and I would do anything for you, too."

The rumbled growl from his chest moved through her. "No putting yourself in danger for me, woman, or I'll tan that ass for you."

A frisson of desire shot through Taamira and straight to her pussy at that image in her head.

"Hmm, you like that idea." Liam nuzzled her neck with his lips, and her body began to tingle at the delicate touches on her neck. "Hold that thought for another day, treacle, because we have a King to entertain."

With that, there was a knock at the door.

Liam pulled back, and she noted he looked unaffected by their moment except she could feel the hard ridge of steel behind his jeans, the knowledge caused her to smirk a little.

"Well, that's one way to kill a mood." Liam laughed as Dane put his head around the door.

"The King of Eyan is here to see you, Taamira."

"Thank you, Dane. Show him in, please."

Dane grinned at her emphasis on the word please and she smiled back.

"Right you are, Princess."

———

THE DOOR OPENED, and King Saud al Kamali walked in followed by two of his guards. Liam hadn't paid too much attention to them downstairs except to make sure they weren't a threat to them. But now as he did, he could see they had been cut from a different cloth to Abdul's guards. There seemed to be none of the aggression from them, just alertness that he would expect.

His attention moved to Taamira's father as he approached. He was not an overly tall man, perhaps around five feet nine inches but his stature didn't seem to matter because the man had a magnetism about him that he seemed to switch on or off at will.

Downstairs in the restaurant, he had gone unnoticed until he wanted to be seen and yet now it was turned all the way up, and he became the centre of the room for most. Not him though, his focus was Taamira, it would always be Taamira.

The King stepped towards his daughter and Liam tensed, which didn't go unnoticed by the King. "My beautiful daughter, let me look at you." He stepped closer, holding his hands to her, and she placed her hands in his.

"Father, you look well."

The politeness grated on Liam's nerves, but he'd let this play out while it wasn't hurting Taamira.

"May we sit?" King Saud requested, and Taamira showed him to a set of chairs around a small glass table in the centre of the room.

The King assessed his daughter and Liam was sure he saw sadness and regret tinge the man's features. "I have missed you, my child."

Taamira went rigid beneath the hand Liam laid on her shoulder. "Perhaps my value should have been considered before, when I was in desperate need of my father to come to my aid."

Her father sighed, and Liam noticed the lines of strain around his eyes as well as the weariness. "I do not expect you to believe me, Taamira, but I authorised the payment of your ransom immediately on hearing the news of your kidnapping. Your brother called me, and I told him to pay whatever it took. And in his defence, Abdul was all set to wire the money from his personal account if I had declined, which I would never have done." The King shook his head, and for some crazy reason, Liam believed this man spoke the truth.

"I do not know what went wrong afterwards, but I would never see you harmed. I know I was not a perfect father, but I do love you. I wish that you believed that. It saddens me greatly that you do not."

"But if you paid it, and Abdul wanted it paid, what went wrong?"

Liam heard the anguish in Taamira's voice and moved closer, laying both his hands on her shoulders for support. She reached up and held onto his fingers as her father watched them.

"I wish I knew, but all I do know is the palace is not the same without you. Your vibrancy, your joy is a loss. Not since the death of your mother has the palace been so joyless, so barren."

Taamira reached for her father's hand and squeezed. "I still miss her, too."

"You are very much like her. It heartens me to see her in you. She refused to marry me the first four times I proposed, you know."

The King's chuckle had Taamira looking up from their hands. "Really? I did not know that. I thought it was an arranged marriage."

"It was, but I knew the moment I saw her that she was the love of my life. My parents raised me to think of women as second to men, but my Nuha would not tolerate that. She told me that only when I proved to her I saw her as equal would I have her heart."

"What did you do?"

Liam heard the interest in his woman's voice and knew she had never heard this story before.

"I wooed her. I listened, and she became my biggest advisor in all things, from government policy to state occasions. She became my world, and then you and Abdul came along, and I did not think my life could be any happier."

The King was animated, but it dropped, and Liam saw genuine grief on his face. "And then she became sick, and she faded from me, and I lost her. I let my grief steal everything she had taught me, everything she had given me. I turned away from you when I should have held you both close.

"Yet while you thrived, Abdul was weaker, and I let him become that. Allowed the people around me to raise my children how they saw fit instead of treasuring the memory of my wife and doing what she would want."

He looked up at Taamira, taking her hands in his and holding them while he looked at her closely. "I failed you and Abdul, and for that, I am truly sorry. Abdul has become a weak man, but I know his heart is the same as it was, I just hope I am not too late. As for you, my beautiful daughter, you're a true leader and I never saw it. You epitomise everything Nuha was, and I see her spirit inside you. I am so proud of the woman you have become."

"Thank you, Daddy." Her voice was clogged with emotion and Liam wanted nothing more than to hold her close.

"I want you to know how proud I am of you and how sorry I am that I allowed this estrangement to last. You will always have a place in the palace, and I fully support the voice you are giving to the women of our country. I know your mother would be so proud too and support you.

"Therefore, I am looking into new laws and some changes to how we do things in Eyan. I want to start small so as not to cause outrage, but I will begin by opening up education to both sexes based on merit. I am also changing the laws around domestic abuse. I would be honoured if you would help me."

Taamira closed the gap between herself and her father, throwing her arms around him and surprising both the King and his guards who froze for second before relaxing.

The look of pure joy on the King's face could not be faked, and Liam glanced at Jack, who shrugged.

"I would love to help, but I have to tell you, I will not be returning to Eyan." She reached back and snagged Liam's hand in hers. "My life is in the UK now, with Liam."

King Saud looked up at Liam, assessing him and Liam held his gaze without flinching. "He looks at you as I once looked at Nuha. Do you love my daughter?"

"With every bone in my body," Liam stated clearly as Taamira brought his hand to her cheek.

"That is all a father can ask. You will bring her to Eyan when it is safe, and we will visit."

The King did not ask, he told Liam it was happening, and Liam let him have that. He had given Taamira her family back in some small way today, and for that reason, he would allow the man to order him around just this once.

"I will when I'm certain it's safe to do so."

King Saud stood, his bearing stable and upright. "Yes, it is not safe at the moment. I fear we have a snake in our beautiful garden. I have my own men looking into it, and if they find anything, they are under orders from me to share the information with you. I want my family back."

"Do you have any leads?" Liam turned his gaze to the King's guard.

"We will send over everything we have to a secure email address."

Liam nodded and watched as the party headed to the door.

Taamira had looped her arm with her father's and stopped to give him a light kiss on his cheek at the door. "Will you watch me give my speech tomorrow?"

Liam heard the uncertainty in her voice and knew it would take time for her to trust her father's change, as it would him.

"I would not miss it. Now, I must speak with my son and rectify the damage I have done to him also."

They watched the King enter the elevator and give them a quick smile before the doors closed, and he was gone.

Liam closed the door tightly and laid his arm around Taamira's shoulder, pulling her close. "That was unexpected."

"It was, and yet for the first time since my mother died, he is acting like the father I remember when I was growing up."

"How old were you when she died?"

"Ten, it was tough because just as I was starting to see the world, she began to fade from it. She had cancer, and it was a long, ravaging process. It was as if I lost both my parents that year."

"I'm glad your father finally saw his mistakes."

"Me too, although I feel cautious. Does that make sense?"

He twirled a lock of her hair in his fingers as he inhaled her sweet scent, not sure if he could love this woman more than he did, and then finding at every turn he could. "It makes perfect sense. Your father hurt you, they all have, and you're protecting your heart from more pain."

Taamira reached up, wrapping her arms around his neck. "I love you."

"I love you, too." He kissed her lightly, dreaming of the day it was just the two of them again.

"Do you need to work?"

Liam nodded regretfully. "I do. We have to finish questioning Scott, and Lopez has some financials for us to look through, plus I have a few new ideas ticking through my brain after today's happenings."

"Okay, I might take a bath and maybe read a book."

"Shall I pop my head in when we order some food, see if you're hungry or do you want to be left alone?"

"No, come get me. I want to eat with you guys."

Liam kissed her once more wishing he could take it deeper but knowing he couldn't. First chance he got, he wanted this woman all to himself.

CHAPTER TWENTY-THREE

TAAMIRA TURNED on her side in the big bed and instantly reached for Liam only to find his side of the bed cold. She sighed, feeling a sense of loss. It had only been a few days that she had shared his bed, but she had already grown accustomed to waking up with him.

He had come to bed around three in the morning, sliding in behind her and gently pulling her body into the hard, warm shield of his arms. A feeling of rightness had settled in her bones, and she had relaxed enough to sleep.

The hours before that, after eating a supper of soup and chicken pesto panini for her and burger and fries for the men, she had retired to her room. Liam had kissed her soundly, telling her he still had a fair bit of work to do but he would be in as soon as he could.

Taamira had not minded, all the work he and the others were doing was for her, to keep her safe and she could never repay them for their kindness, but she would try.

It had been after midnight, and her brain was still playing over the meeting with her father. The change in him had been profound, but as she had let her mind drift, she realised it was not as shocking as she first thought. Memories of a man who had walked with her in the garden showing her different types of flowers returned.

Her mind drifting, forgotten thoughts of him smiling at her as he sat with her mother at dinner, his hand resting on the top of his wife's much smaller one came to her. Her mother had been a great beauty, having a sweet nature but as she let her mind open to old pictures in her head, she got the sense that her mother and father had been real partners. Best friends, almost nary a day went when they were not together.

Had that man who had adored her mother so profoundly suddenly seen the light and come back to them or was it all a ruse? Taamira hated that she did not know, that she distrusted so deeply she could not take her own father at his word, especially as she so wanted to, or maybe it was because she wanted it so badly.

He and her brother had hurt her in such a way she was not sure she would ever fully trust them again. Had her father and brother authorised her captor's payment? If they had, what had gone wrong? Who hated her enough to want to see those atrocities done to her? The thoughts had gone full circle around and again until her eyes were gritty from tiredness, her brain like scrambled egg.

Only when she was safe in Liam's arms had she finally drifted off to sleep. Flipping on her back, Taamira saw it was ten-thirty. She had slept later than she wanted, but as her speech was not until tonight and she had little else to do, she was not concerned.

Slipping from the bed, she padded to the bathroom and relieved her bladder before brushing her teeth and then stepping into the shower.

Quickly washing her hair and body, shaving her legs and under-arms, she stepped out and almost screamed when she saw a hulking mass in the doorway.

Liam smirked and moved closer, his eyes running over her body, holding out the towel for her. "Not the kind of scream I was going for, Princess."

"You scared me. How can a man your size be so silent on his feet?"

"Ballet lessons."

Taamira turned in his arms and stared up at him as her hands came to rest on his hard chest. The hard muscle under her hands had her body tingling with desire. "You took ballet lessons?" Her voice was huskier as she asked the question.

"Of course not, treacle. It's just part of the job. You learn not to make a noise if you want to stay breathing."

"Oh." Taamira could hardly remember what they had been talking about as his rough hands that brought her so much pleasure lightly caressed her skin where her thighs and buttocks met.

"You can't look at me like that, Taamira." His words were harsh with need.

Taamira wanted him with a visceral desire that was hard and fast, flooding her body with heady endorphins and making her bold. Her hand moved to the denim-covered ridge of steel that was his cock. "Why not?"

"Makes me want to fuck you on this counter."

"What's stopping you?"

She heard the growl in his throat as his mouth came down on hers, hard and desperate as he lifted her, his hands on her ass. Taamira wound her arms around his neck and kissed him back as if her life depended on it. The towel was whipped from her body, the soft skin of his white t-shirt rubbing against her nipples in delicious friction.

"Fuck, treacle, I need you."

The gravelly sound in his voice had her desperate to be filled by him, knowing only he could make her body sing.

"I need you, too."

Taamira found herself sat on the edge of the vanity, Liam's hungry eyes devouring her as his hand swept adoringly from her cheek down her neck, over her breasts. His thumbs rubbed her nipples in a circle until she was crazy from wanting him.

Liam's hot breath on her tender nubs made her body tingle before he sucked one into his mouth torturing her even more. Training her eyes on him, she reached for his zip, releasing his cock, and stroking the velvety hardness. Power flooded her as he threw his head back and moaned his pleasure before his eyes were back on her.

Stepping closer, he lined his cock up with her pussy and drove himself inside her as she watched pleasure cross his handsome face, mirroring what she knew was on hers.

His movements were fast and brutal and just what she needed. Taamira wrapped her legs around him as his hands teased her body until she was mindlessly writhing.

His big hands on her hips gripped her as she reached for his head, kissing him as the first ripples of her climax rushed through her body before she cried out her orgasm into the kiss they shared.

"Fuck, Taamira. God, you feel like heaven."

His movements became jerky as he spilt his seed inside her, his head buried in her neck and she held on like he was her island in a storm.

His breathing heavy, he pulled back, kissing her softly and languidly before he looked at her with an apology. "We didn't use protection, Princess. I'm so sorry." He pulled from her body and tucked himself away, not looking at her.

Taamira took his face in her hands and forced him to look at her, his beloved face holding so much love for her. "Liam, we are in this together and would it be so bad if we created a child?" Her heart was in her throat as she waited for his reply.

He did not make her wait, never one to play games with her feelings. "I'd love nothing more than to fill your belly with my babies." His hand rubbed a small circle on her belly. "But I want it to be something we decide, not something that happens by accident."

"I love that, but if it has happened, then it was fate, and fate brought me you, so I trust what she has in store for me."

His eyes went soft as his knuckles grazed her cheek. "Have I told you how much I love you today?"

Taamira looked up and left, her finger on her cheek as she pretended to think before she shook her head. "No, I don't believe you have."

"How remiss of me. I love you, Princess Treacle, more than you will ever know. You have changed my life. Made me see beyond my grief for my friend, brought me a sense of belonging that I never had before."

"It's only been a week," she said with a watery laugh, his words meaning so much to her.

Liam shook his head. "Not for me. I think I started falling in love with you the minute you told me you hated my shirt. It just took me this long to recognise it, to see what my life could be like if I just stopped fighting it and gave you my heart."

"Liam." Taamira blinked at the tears of joy his words brought.

"Once this is over, we'll visit your Eyan and you can show me where you grew up, share it all with me. I want our children to know the beauty of you and where you came from."

This man was slaying her with his words, knitting all the wounds her family caused back together with his love and care for her heart. "I would love that, and if we did make a child today, I will know that he or she came from a moment I will treasure all my days."

"I actually didn't come in here for this, although it was a very nice detour."

"Oh, what did you want to tell me?" Taamira jumped down as Liam handed her a towel for her hair and body.

"Evelyn, Astrid, and Laverne are here to spend some time with you. Alex thought it might be nice if the women got ready with you."

"I don't think I know Laverne or Astrid," Taamira said as she pulled on underwear.

"They work with Evelyn, and both are nice girls."

Jealousy wove through her brain like an ugly snake. "Oh." Her single word was harsh and proud, and she hated that she had reacted like that.

Liam moved closer, a grin on his face as he caught her around her waist. "They are nice girls," he began, and she crossed her arms and glared, "you are everything, so stop with the jealousy, Princess. I've never touched any of the Zenobi girls, nor do I want to. Everyone ceased to exist for me the minute I met a certain pushy princess."

Taamira relaxed, feeling foolish for her behaviour. "I am sorry, that was a kneejerk reaction. I know you would never hurt me like that."

"Don't apologise, treacle, I kind of like you all territorial over me, but I draw the line at you peeing on my leg."

"Eww, Liam, that is gross."

His smile reassured her that she hadn't ruined the moment with her green-eyed monster routine.

"Anyway, the girls are going to be here in ten minutes. Evelyn has a host of things planned for you. I'll be working with Jack and Blake going over tonight's plans again."

"Did Scott tell you anything useful?"

"Not really, he was paid to take the photo and post it online and then was told to meet them here. It turns out he has a gambling addiction we had no clue about and is in debt to some not so nice people."

"What will happen to him now?"

"He'll be charged with breaking a few privacy laws and stripped of his license. He'll be lucky if he gets anything better than shopping centre security jobs from here on out."

"Is it silly that I feel bad for him?"

His hand played through her hair as he gazed at her. "No, Princess, it is part of who you are. You forgive, your inert kindness is what makes me love you. So not silly, just don't expect me to do the same."

He kissed her slowly, the depth of his emotion showed in every second of his kiss and she wondered how she had lived without this man in her life and concluded she hadn't really. He had given her so much—friends, love, family, and a future full of it all. They just needed to put all of this behind them so they could move to the happy ever after part.

CHAPTER TWENTY-FOUR

TAAMIRA DID NOT KNOW how Evelyn had known an afternoon with these three women had been precisely what she needed, but she was glad that she had. On first meeting Lavern and Astrid, she had been uneasy, tense in the presence of such beautiful, confident women. She waited for the nasty jibes and veiled compliments that were really digs at her appearance or her beliefs but none of those things had happened.

Laverne was probably five feet five inches, and slim with long light brown hair, shot through with gold and caramel highlights, and big brown eyes, but it was the smattering of freckles across her nose and over her cheeks that took her from beautiful to damn right stunning. She had a girl next door innocence that was endearing but in a package that was so much more the average.

Astrid, by contrast, was probably five feet ten inches tall, with flawless porcelain skin, and rosy pink cheeks. Her silvery blue eyes slightly turned up at the outer edges giving her sultry appearance, pouty full lips, and a smile that instantly relaxed her, long wavy blonde hair that seemed to have streaks of pure gold when she moved her head.

Both women were far more than nice, and had she known what they looked like before she met them, she feared she would have had a much bigger freak out when Liam mentioned them. She was glad she had buried that and now found she had two more people who could potentially become friends to her.

"I have to say, when I heard Liam was dating a princess, I was a little surprised. It hardly seems like a perfect match," Astrid began and Taamira bristled a little, regret flooding her that she had let her guard down too quickly, "but having seen you two together, and the way you look at each other, I think you're absolutely perfect for each other."

Taamira relaxed, glad she had not fired a response at Astrid too quickly and ruined her fledgling friendships. "I've never met a man like him. He makes me feel like I can own the world, that either he will stand by me while I go and get it, or he will bring it to me on a silver platter." Taamira looked away, embarrassed by her honesty.

"That's how Alex makes me feel," Evelyn admitted.

Laverne groaned. "Please stop with the blissed-up love talk. Some of us have to rely on a B.O.B for our fun."

Taamira had recently learned that a B.O.B was a battery-operated boyfriend, or vibrator, to use its real name.

"It's not about just the sex, although the sex is phenomenal," Evelyn winked at Taamira as she said it. "It's about a partnership where it's you and him against the world. That no matter what happens on this planet, he'll have your back and you'll have his."

"Well, I don't think that's on the cards for me," Astrid said and grinned as she stood and went to the plate of cut fruit that they had sent up.

As soon as the girls had arrived, they had taken over Jack's suite, which was next door to the one she was using, and they currently had it set up as mission control.

Jack had grumbled a little but quickly moved his stuff out of the way so they had space. Now there was a rack with four dresses for that evening, make-up and hair paraphernalia, glasses of bubbly, chocolate covered fruit, and face masks.

Astrid had painted Taamira's nails for her and Evelyn had done Laverne's, and now that they had dried, they were switching. As they debated what colours would best go with their dresses, she smiled at the easy camaraderie she had with these women. How had she gone her entire life without these sorts of friendships? Taamira knew she was not entrenched with them as she could tell the bond between these three had been forged with blood and tears, but she was never on the outside looking in, she was part of the group.

"So, tell me about your country. Is it as beautiful as I've heard?" Laverne asked as she pulled the nail polish brush over Evelyn's nail.

Taamira looked up from adding a topcoat to Astrid's left hand the coral colour a perfect tone for her skin colouring. "It is incredibly beautiful. We have acres and acres of lemon and olive groves, the sea is the clearest you have ever seen, and the sand on the beaches is a perfect white. The spice markets fill the air with lush aromatics, and the vibrant colour of the fruits and vegetable traders alongside the jewel colours of the bolts of silk is a joy to the senses."

"It sounds like heaven."

"It is, and it is not. The place is beauty beyond compare, but the palace itself is like living in a wasp's nest."

"Do you think you will go back at all?" Astrid asked as she put her hand back under the UV light to finish drying her nails.

"I want to show Liam my country. The people of my land are wonderful, the market traders, the restaurant owners, all of the real people, not the ones who think they are above everyone else because they wake up under satin sheets every day."

"Sounds serious between you." Evelyn wiggled her eyebrows.

"It is, he told me he loves me, that he wants us to make a family one day." Taamira shared her joy, wanting to talk about it with others; her excitement spilling over.

"What? This is huge. Why didn't you tell me immediately?" Evelyn demanded with a huge grin.

Taamira looked to the other two women who seemed equally excited for her or perhaps for Liam. "I did not think it would interest you."

"Are you crazy, woman? I live for this kind of thing. Tell me everything."

Taamira told them a little of what had happened and exulting in their honest joy for her.

"This is wonderful. I can't wait for everyone to get partnered up so we can have parties with more women attending. The Eidolon men are great, but the testosterone is ridiculous." Evelyn laughed as she looked at Laverne and Astrid. "You need to get yourselves a man so we can drag you into our blissed-up caravan of love."

Laverne and Astrid looked aghast.

"Not on your life, I don't need or want a man, thanks very much," Astrid stated.

"I thought you and Jack had a vibe," Taamira stated quietly.

"No way, that man makes me want to stab myself in the eye with a rusty knife every time I see him. He may be ridiculously hot, but he's an arrogant, self-centred, egotistical, alpha asshole," Astrid announced

Everyone went silent for as she had been speaking, Jack had walked in behind her and now stood with his arms crossed over his chest, an arched eyebrow and cheeky smirk playing on his face.

"He's behind me, isn't he?" Astrid groaned and turned to find Jack behind her with one eyebrow raised.

"You think I'm hot?"

"Urgh, typical you only notice that word."

"Oh, I noticed all of them, Astrid, I just choose not to listen to your hormonal ramblings."

The women drew in a harsh breath as he said the word hormonal, knowing he'd made a fatal mistake.

Astrid rose like a graceful ballerina and prowled to him, and Taamira stared in fascination as the two beautiful and deadly people glared at each other. "What did you say?"

"You heard me, Astrid, or is the knowledge that I'd never touch you like that clouding your brain?"

"If you ever tried to touch me, I'd cut off your balls and feed them to the pigs," Astrid replied.

"Keep telling yourself that, sweetheart, we both know different." With that, he turned, grabbed his Tuxedo from the hanger on the wardrobe, and walked out of the room.

Taamira looked at Evelyn and Laverne who were staring at Astrid.

"Why do I feel like I need a cigarette or something? That was hot, even insulting each other you two throw some major chemistry," Laverne said as she fanned herself.

Astrid glared at her. "Shut up."

Laverne and Evelyn laughed and dropped the subject, but Taamira wondered if there was way more to that little exchange than anyone knew.

With the tension over they continued getting ready, doing hair and make-up before slipping into their dresses, or in Astrid's case a black, backless jumpsuit. She would be helping Mitch with over-watch as she was a sniper, which was a surprise to Taamira and, therefore, a dress was not practical.

Glancing in the mirror she was happy with what she saw, confident even, the tiny flutter of butterflies the only sign of nerves about her upcoming speech.

The dress was sapphire blue chiffon, with long flowing sleeves of a single layer chiffon with gold embroidery and golden cuffs at her wrists. The layers and layers of chiffon that dropped from a wide intricate gold band at her waist fell to the floor with no adornment. The neckline was a keyhole style which showed off a good amount of cleavage without seeming cheap or too daring. Crystals and pearls adorned the shoulder and neckline. The headband she wore in her hair was gold with a single teardrop sapphire on the centre of her forehead.

"You look absolutely stunning."

Taamira looked up to see Liam standing behind her in the mirror; the other women now nowhere in sight. He looked so handsome in a black tuxedo, white shirt, and black cummerbund. He took her breath away every time he looked at her; she caught her breath to think he was hers.

"You look very dashing."

Taamira turned and saw the admiration in his eyes as he rested his hands on her upper arms.

"Are you ready?"

She put her hand on her belly as nerves assailed her. This speech would change everything, but she had the backing of the man she loved and perhaps even the father she thought she had lost. "Am I doing the right thing? Making this speech, speaking out against the traditions of my country?"

He looked at her intently. "Does it feel right?"

"I don't know. What if I mess it up?"

"You won't, you know that speech inside out and backwards. What is your heart saying?"

"That I need to do this."

"Then follow your heart and whatever happens, happens. I will support you one hundred and ten per cent. I think what you're doing for the women of your country is brave and from what your father said of her, your mother would be incredibly proud of you as well."

Tears burned, and she swallowed them down. "I hope so."

"I know so. Just go out there and speak from the heart and don't worry about anything else. The team will be watching the entire time to make sure nobody gets anywhere near you."

"What about you?"

"I'll be no further than two feet from you the entire time, except when you make your speech, and the team will be in the crowd. I'll be in the wings."

"I'm not worried about me. I just don't want anyone to get hurt because of me."

Liam cupped her cheeks and tilted her head, so she was looking into his beautiful blue eyes. "Nobody is going to get hurt because of you. Whatever happens, this is not your doing. You're innocent in this."

Taamira nodded, not quite accepting his words but wanting to appease the man she loved.

"Now give me that smile I love so much."

Taamira smiled at him, not helping herself where he was concerned.

"That's better."

He offered her his arm which she took, burying the unsettling nerves deep as she put on her public persona.

CHAPTER TWENTY-FIVE

LIAM CAST his eye up and around the vast room, looking for the different members of his team when all he wanted to do was gaze at the vision in front of him. Her beauty took his breath away, but it was the way she turned to him when her nerves had been getting the better of her that made him feel like the luckiest bastard alive.

He spotted Alex and Evelyn looking like the original power couple talking with a couple of movie stars. He knew Jack was to his left, not two feet away with Laverne on his arm as they shadowed them. Zack and Dane were over by the band that was playing some sort of classical shit he hated. K and Zin were standing at opposite ends of the bar nursing drinks and fighting off women, successfully he might add.

Mitch was high up in the roof, his sights continually watching them, with Astrid watching his back. Blake, who was the most experienced with high-value targets and personal protection, was backstage ensuring nobody put anything they shouldn't near the entrance to the stage.

"Prime Minister, it is so good to see you."

Liam watched Taamira hold out her hand to the leader of Canada.

"Your Royal Highness, so good to see you again." The Prime Minister, a slightly unattractive woman in her late fifties, took Taamira's hand and shook it firmly.

The two made small talk and Liam zoned out the conversation when they started talking about economic growth. It was impressive how Taamira could handle herself in any given situation with ease and grace. However, his sole focus was her protection and he kept a calm eye on the people around them, noting movie stars, government officials, leaders of countries, royalty, and heads of industry. There were so many high-value targets in this room—it was a terrorist's dream come true.

What stopped that was a small army of personal protection in the room, every one of these people had security with them, some had small teams of one or two, others had larger teams like they did, but all kept their focus on keeping their principle safe.

Liam sighed as he caught sight of King Saud as he entered the room with his son Prince Abdul, and a woman he presumed was the prince's wife, their security not two steps away from them.

Lifting his arm slightly, he spoke into the mic. "Bert and Ernie are in the room."

Resounding replies of, "Copy" came over the headset.

He had laughed when Jack decided on that moniker for the King and his son. He knew Taamira loved them both despite what they had done. Although the King had explained what he had done to Liam, it wasn't enough.

If it had been his daughter, he would've been on the first flight to make sure she was okay in person and heads would have fucking rolled for a mistake like that, but what did he know, he had no children. A smile twitched his lips at the thought that maybe he could have and instead of terrifying him, it had him smiling to himself.

When he had realised what he had done, taking her like an animal in the bathroom with no thought of using protection, he'd felt like a scumbag piece of crap. Taamira's reaction had been just what he needed. She would never know how much she enriched his life.

Taamira began to move towards the Prince of Monaco. Liam snagged a glass of fruit juice from a passing waiter and handed it to her. "Here, drink, I don't want you getting dehydrated."

Her eyes sparkled as she took several small sips of the juice. "I can't drink too much, or I will need to use the ladies' room.

"So, use it. I won't let anyone in, and Laverne can go with you."

"You truly think of everything, don't you?"

Liam chuckled as he took the half-empty glass back from her and gave it to a passing waitress.

"Sister."

Liam groaned as he heard her brother's voice to their left. He had seen him coming but knew they couldn't avoid him all night so had distracted her from her nerves with the juice.

He saw Taamira take a steadying breath before she turned with a graceful smile on her lips.

"Abdul, Fawzaana, Father, nice to see you again."

Her father stepped forward and took her hands, holding them out to her sides as he looked at her. "Don't you look like a vision."

"Thank you," Taamira said politely, but Liam heard the guarded-ness in her voice.

She was still unsure if this was going to last or if it was even real.

She looked to her brother's wife with a smile that didn't reach her eyes. "Fawzaana, you look well."

Liam watched the other woman with an eagle eye seeing the tightness of her jaw and the calculation in her cold eyes before she hid both and offered Taamira a sweet smile. "You look..." Her eyes moved over Taamira slowly, and Liam saw the woman he loved still as she waited for the verbal put down he knew was coming.

That was never happening again on his watch. "She looks breath-taking, doesn't she?"

His words earned him the interest of both Abdul and Fawzaana, but he knew the King was watching Taamira. He didn't like being involved in this family drama; it meant he wasn't concentrating on any potential threat. Thank God he had his team to watch his back, while Taamira only had him at that moment.

"Yes, breathtaking," Fawzaana said slowly before she glared at him.

He held her gaze, showing her exactly who she was dealing with at that moment, and it was only moments before she lowered hers.

"Are you my sister's guard or her boyfriend tonight?" Abdul enquired with a sneer at the word boyfriend.

Liam knew Taamira loved this man, but he didn't like him and probably never would, but he would hold his tongue as best he could. "I will always be protector, lover, and partner to my Princess." Liam saw the look of approval on the King's face and didn't give a shit about it, all he cared about was her.

"As I will be yours," she stated, reaching for his hand.

Abdul said nothing for a moment. "Then, I welcome you." He bowed slightly.

Fawzaana gasped, her look of anger barely contained. "Such an outrage to speak with such frankness in public."

"It is what this family needs more of. I am sick of the sniping and the hateful words uttered with false smiles. Liam is laying his cards on the table, standing behind my daughter, and that is commendable. Perhaps you could learn something from him, Abdul."

The King's words were met with silence until Abdul bowed his head. "Perhaps you are correct, Father. I did not mean any harm, Liam, and I am sure neither did my wife." He gave his wife a pointed look, but she mutinously kept her eyes away.

"No harm to me, just as long as there's a smile on Taamira's face, I'm good."

Taamira leaned closer and linked her arm with his. "It is time I head back for my speech. Father, Abdul, Fawzaana." She tipped her head, and they made their escape.

"Thank you," she whispered as they moved towards the stage.

"Is it wrong to say it was an absolute pleasure?"

Taamira giggled, and he grinned back. Her smile had him wanting to harness the moon just to be on the receiving end of it.

As they moved behind the curtain, his shoulders tensed. This was the most dangerous part of the evening, when she would be out in front of all these people on her own, with a fucking spotlight shining on her, and him not close enough to do a damn thing to protect her.

"Digby is on the move," he spoke into his wrist, letting everyone know they were minutes out from the speech. Taamira had chosen her own code name, and he laughed when she'd chosen the name of his donkey.

Blake met them and nodded. "Princess." He turned to Liam. "This area is clean. I swept it myself."

Liam lifted his chin in acknowledgement. "Mitch, you have eyes on the stage?"

"Good copy, I have eyes on."

"Everyone in position?" Liam asked as the Prime Minister of Spain introduced the reason for the conference and gave a small speech before he announced Taamira as the guest speaker.

A series of confirmations came through, and his gut still churned. Something was off, everything was too smooth, too flawless and it was making him jumpy. Although he had to admit in these circumstances, he'd always worry because he was about to put his whole world in danger and could do nothing to stop it, short of wrapping her in cotton wool and hiding her away for the rest of her life, which would result in her slowly dying.

He heard the Prime Minister wrapping up and took Taamira's hands in his. "If you have even the slightest doubt or see anything that makes you unsure, you get off that stage. Do you hear me?"

"Yes, I hear you. Do not worry, Liam, it will all be fine."

Her name was announced, so he didn't respond. Straightening her shoulders, Taamira walked on to the stage with a huge smile.

Liam noted Jack in the opposite wing, watching her earnestly, his eyes moving between the stage and the crowd. Liam was doing the same, although it was hard to see properly with the lights shining at them, even though he stayed out of sight.

He saw the audience entranced as Taamira spoke, enslaving them with her passion for her subject.

"All clear," Mitch murmured.

Liam watched King Saud, along with Abdul and Fawzaana, who were close to the stage. The King looked proud and surprisingly so did Abdul, but Fawzaana looked satisfied. That surprised him and instantly put his guard up further.

"Keep an eye on Abdul's wife. I don't like the way she's looking at Taamira."

Liam looked around quickly for Abdul's guard and didn't find him anywhere. He should have been next to this principle, but he'd left his post. Their discussions with the King's guard hadn't helped any, so they still had no real knowledge of precisely where the threat lay.

"Find Mustafa, Abdul's guard, he's left his post."

Liam stepped forward, seconds away from dragging Taamira off the stage when he saw Mustafa, but he was too late. The man already had his gun in his hand and was raising it towards Taamira.

His feet were already moving him across the stage as he yelled, "Gun!"

With a mighty leap, he pushed Taamira to the ground as shocked gasps rent the air and two bullets slammed into the side of his chest, where his vest had no cover. He hit the ground hard but shoved himself up in time to see Taamira's terrified face as Blake and Jack dragged her to safety as she fought them to get to him.

Satisfied she was safe, he let the pain and blackness envelop him as he passed out. His last thought was that he could die happy knowing his friends would take care of the woman he loved.

CHAPTER TWENTY-SIX

TAAMIRA KICKED and screamed as Jack lifted her bodily and dragged her away from Liam, tears streaming down her face as she screamed his name. People were running, yelling, but she didn't care about any of it, all that mattered was Liam lying on the ground bleeding after he had saved her.

A sob ripped from her throat, and Jack held her tight to his chest, offering her comfort as he tried to shield her from everyone. She heard him speak, snapping out orders to his people.

"Is the gunman dead?" Jack asked, and she sobbed harder. "I need this place fucking locked down. Nobody leaves this hotel until I'm sure we have these fuckers banged to rights."

Jack pulled back and held her upper arms firmly as she wiped her tears away. "The paramedics are taking Liam to La Paz by helicopter. His wounds are serious, Taamira. Do you want me to take you to your room where you'll be safe, or to the hospital?"

Taamira was shocked that he was giving her a choice, not that there was one, the only place she wanted to be was near Liam.

"With Liam." Her voice was still shaky, but she was under control a little now, she could fall apart later.

Jack nodded, a look of pride on his face. "We'll meet them there. They need the room in the chopper to work on Liam."

His words filled her with fear, and she knew he was trying to prepare her for the worst.

"Fine." It was not fine, nothing would be fine again until she knew Liam would be okay.

Twenty minutes later, she was in a private relative's room with Jack and Blake, waiting for an update on the man she loved.

Too wired to sit, she paced the room, jumping when the door opened and Alex and Evelyn walked in. Evelyn walked straight up to her and wrapped her in a tight hug. It was to offer comfort, but the only thing that would do that right now was Liam's arms around her.

"Any news?" Alex asked as Evelyn released her. Alex looked devastated, as did Jack.

"No, nothing yet. They took him straight into surgery."

Over the next few hours, the room filled with people—Blake, Mitch, Zack, Zin, Kanan, Dane, Astrid, Laverne—every one of them looked absolutely worried sick for their friend, and she realised just how loved Liam was.

Astrid and Laverne had barely left her side, Laverne having brought her a change of clothes that she was loathe to change into. This dress had Liam's blood on it, and yet, even that tiny piece of him was better than nothing.

Anger filled her as the impotence of the situation became too much for her to bear. "Who did this to him?" Her eyes were trained on Jack, knowing if anyone had that information, it was him.

He held her gaze without flinching away from her direct question and with regret answered. "Mustafa, your brother's head of security."

Taamira slapped a hand to her mouth as bile raced its way up her throat and she dove for the door, hoping to make it to the ladies' room before she threw up.

"Go with her," Jack demanded behind her.

Taamira barely made it to the toilet before she was retching the meagre contents of her stomach into the pan. She felt a gentle hand on her back, another holding her hair out of the way as she sagged to the wall beside her. A wet tissue was thrust at her and she took it, turning to see Evelyn, Astrid, and Laverne, who had handed her the tissue, waiting for her.

The girls surrounded her, holding her up with their arms and their gentle words of reassurance as she broke down for the second time. "I cannot lose him."

"Liam is strong, Taamira. You can't think like that. He needs you to fight for him now, to stay strong."

"I do not know if I can."

Astrid lifted her head so she was looking her directly in the eye. "Yes, you can. We'll help you. Now, get changed and wash your face. Your family just arrived, and we need him to see you strong."

Those words had Taamira's backbone turning to steel. Her family was here after one of their guards had shot the man she loved. She did not think so. Snatching up the clothes, she ripped off her dress, throwing it to the ground, all of her modesty gone in her haste to give her family a dressing down. She pulled on the jeans Liam loved, as well as the cashmere sweater and suede boots.

Washing her face, she pulled her hair into a ponytail and wiped the streaks of mascara from her cheeks before she rinsed her mouth and took the mint Evelyn handed her with a wink.

"Atta girl."

Opening the door, she saw Alex and Blake waiting for them to walk her back to the relative's room which was now full of her family and friends.

"Taamira." Her father rushed to take her hands, but she pulled them away. Hurt flashed in his eyes before he spoke again. "Is there any news?"

Taamira crossed her arms and glared at the people who should have protected her always and had failed, and now through their own ignorance had allowed one of their most trusted to commit a crime that could change her life forever.

"Why are you here?"

She saw her father's face fall and fought to keep from going to him.

"Taamira!" scolded her brother.

She turned her glare on him. "What? I have no clue why you would be here. When I was attacked, you could not be bothered, so why now? Come to make sure your man hit his mark or maybe to kill me as I was the intended target?" She fought to keep her voice even as she spoke those words.

Her brother paled. "How could you think such a thing? We are as shocked and disgusted as anyone. We had no idea Mustafa was involved in anything like that. We love you."

"That is the problem. You did not know because you are lazy and entitled. It is your job to secure the safety of your country, and yet you do not even know what is going on inside your own home. As for love, you need to go away and learn what love is. Love is always, and I mean always, being there for the people you love, it is showing them they have worth, caring for their feelings, and putting them before yourself. You do not show that, and you certainly do not have it." She cast her eyes to Fawzaana as she said the last.

The woman had the grace to look away, sadness in her eyes.

"You are upset. We should leave you."

Her brother backtracked towards the door with Fawzaana, but her father stayed and looked at her with pain in his eyes. "Everything you say is right, we have failed you, and I will fix this. I will make this right. Please know that Liam is in my prayers, as are you." He turned to Jack. "Please keep me updated."

Jack shrugged. "Not up to me. Taamira is the one in charge of that."

King Saud dipped his head and left the room and Taamira sagged, Mitch catching her as she did. He led her to the couch and sat her down beside him, his arm staying around her shoulders.

"You did good, Princess. Liam would be proud of you."

She offered him a wan smile. "I hope so."

"I know so."

HOURS LATER, a doctor walked into the room and looked around at them all. "Who is next of kin?" Evelyn translated for them.

"She is," Jack pointed at Taamira as Evelyn said something in Spanish to the doctor who nodded and moved towards her.

"Mr Hayes received injuries to his liver, kidney, and right lung. We had to remove part of his liver and the right kidney as the damage was too extensive. His lung is now functioning after it collapsed, but he is not out of the woods, and will have a long recovery." He had switched to English, and even though his accent was strong, Taamira was grateful that she was able to communicate with him directly.

"But he will be okay?"

"The next forty-eight hours will tell us more. Once he wakes, we can ensure there were no neurological injuries caused by the lack of oxygen to his brain."

"Brain injury? You never mentioned a brain injury." Taamira gasped as she held tight to Mitch and Laverne who were either side of her.

"He didn't receive a brain injury as such, but his heart stopped twice on the operating table, and we can't be sure that he didn't sustain any damage while we got his heart started again."

Taamira bit her lip as she tried to fight the tears and be strong. "Can I see him?"

"He is in the ICU, so it's one at a time and only for a ten minute period. Rest is what his body needs right now."

"Thank you."

The doctor squeezed her hand his kind eyes promising nothing. "I will send the nurse to get you when we have him settled in a room.

He left the room, and it remained silent as everyone took in the seriousness of the news. Liam was alive, but he had a fight on his hands, and she and everyone in that room would be fighting for him.

One thing she did know was that this was a family of value, one that would live and die for each other and had no trouble showing the world they cared. This was what she wanted, and she needed to make sure they knew how grateful she was for them. "Thank you for being here with me."

Jack glanced at her. "Nowhere else we would be. Liam is our brother, and that makes you family, too."

"I love him so much. I cannot bear the thought of..." She could not finish.

Jack crouched in front of her, his elbows resting on his thighs. "We know you love him, and he loves you, too. You've given him something to fight for, Taamira, so you be strong for him, and we'll be strong for you. When this is over, and Liam is being a pain in the ass again, we'll still be doing it because he's going to make it."

Taamira nodded, strengthened by his words.

CHAPTER TWENTY-SEVEN

THE DOOR to the private hospital room opened, and Taamira looked up from where she sat beside Liam's bed. Three days had passed since Liam had been shot and he still hadn't woken. She still hadn't got to see those beautiful blue eyes she loved so much. The doctor said it was not unusual after such a massive trauma to the body, but she could see in his eyes every time he did his rounds that he was growing increasingly concerned about his patient.

"Have you had any sleep at all these past few days?" Evelyn asked as she moved towards her, handing her a large cardboard cup full of coffee from the coffee shop down the road.

"I slept in the chair."

Evelyn tutted and looked at Alex behind her. "Tell her she needs to go and get some real sleep."

Alex grinned as he moved to Evelyn, slipping his hand around her waist, and pulling her flush to his body. "Would you leave if it was me in that bed?"

Evelyn shrugged. "Probably not."

"There you go. If Taamira wants to be with Liam, let her."

"Fine. But she needs to eat."

Taamira took a sip of the coffee, the soothing, dark liquid hitting her empty belly, warming from the inside out. Evelyn was right, she needed to keep her strength up.

When Liam came home, she would want to look after him, and she needed to stay healthy for that. Her eyes pricked with fear as emotion and tiredness hit her.

Evelyn put her arm around her shoulders. "Hey, come on. He's going to be okay. Liam is strong, he won't leave you when he just found you."

Taamira sniffed and pulled herself together. "I know he is. Let me just wash my face, and we will get some food."

"Good, Mitch and Waggs are on their way in so they can sit with Liam and keep him company while we eat a quick bite."

Taamira's worry eased a little knowing his friends would be with him in case he woke. She did not want him to be alone. Giving her face a quick splash of water, she re-fixed her ponytail and added some lip balm before meeting Evelyn and Alex back in the room.

She looked up as Waggs and Mitch came in, and both men came and gave her hugs.

"How's the big guy doing?"

"Holding his own according to the doctor." She gazed down at the man she loved; he looked so pale, and yet he still filled the room, even unconscious he was not shrunken and weak. He looked strong and vital, but the cannula in his hand pumping him with fluids and antibiotics said differently.

"That's good. Before we know it, he'll be driving everyone crazy again as we try and figure out what the hell he's saying with his cockney rubbish," Waggs said and laughed, and Taamira smiled.

"We're gonna grab some food for this one." Evelyn jerked her thumb at Taamira. "Will you sit with him while we do?"

Mitch gave Taamira a massive grin as he put his arm around her. "Get some food. While you're gone, I'll whisper in Liam's ear about how I intend to charm you away from him, and the bugger will soon wake his ass up."

She chuckled lightly at his antics, appreciating how they were all trying to keep her spirits up.

As she went to turn left to the hospital canteen, Alex and Evelyn drew her towards the rear exit. "Where are we going?"

"Hospital food is no good for you. You need proper food. Alex found this little bistro that makes wonderful light lunches. You can get some fresh air, eat, and then be refreshed when you go back."

Taamira turned back to the room not really wanting to leave the hospital, wanting to be close to Liam.

Evelyn dragged her by her arm down the hall. "If Liam so much as twitches, Waggs will call us."

Taamira paused and then nodded. Evelyn was right, if anything happened, they would call her; she knew that.

Allowing herself to be shuffled along, she went into the bistro with Alex and Evelyn and smiled when she saw Pax and Blake.

Pax immediately stood and wrapped her in a tight hug. Her comfort fortifying Taamira. "What are you doing here?"

Pax sat back down as they all took seats. "I needed to be here for you, so I flew out late last night."

Taamira was touched by that more than she could even enunciate. "Wow, thank you."

"How is he?" Pax asked as she held Blake's hand under the table.

"He is holding his own, his vitals are good, all of the early tests and signs are good. It is just a waiting game now."

Pax smiled. "These things can't be rushed."

They all gave orders to the waitress as she came over, Taamira only ordering fruit juice and a light seafood salad.

The conversation was light, Pax giving her an update on Digby which had her smiling and missing home, not home in Eyan but the home she had with Liam. The food was pleasant, and she ate more than she thought she would, obviously hungrier than she realised.

"Have you heard from your family today?" Alex asked.

Her brother and father had called daily requesting updates on both her and Liam. Neither had flown home, opting to stay in

Geneva until they knew Liam was on the mend. Taamira had spoken to her father twice, and he seemed to have genuinely changed and wanted to be her father again.

It just wasn't that simple, although Taamira could feel her heart softening to him. Abdul had sent baskets of fruit to her, and she had called to thank him. He had sounded different, but she still could not help but think her brother was lost.

The brother she had now was flailing as he tried to be the man he could be, no should have been, if he had continued to have a good influence, versus the man who had been moulded by misogynistic men who believed women had no value.

She hoped he found his way and maybe when she had more energy, she would help him, but for now, the only strength she did have she reserved for the man who lay in a hospital bed because he had literally jumped in front of a bullet for her.

"My father called, asked if he could do anything."

"He seems to be really trying," Pax said softly.

"I know, it just is not that simple. A lot of hurt has passed under the bridge, and it will be a long time before clear water runs smooth between us."

Pax took her hand. "I understand, honey, believe me, I do. When this is all over, remind me to tell you about my parents. Now, they're a pair."

Taamira was intrigued, but she knew it would wait, she wanted to get back to Liam.

"You're itching to go, aren't you?" Evelyn asked.

"I do not like to leave him."

"I understand, let Alex take care of the bill and then we'll all walk back together."

"I can get this." Alex frowned at her, making it clear that she would not be paying the bill. "Fine."

As the five of them walked back into the hospital, she quickened her pace wanting to be with Liam again.

Walking into the room, the band around her chest eased as she saw him lying precisely as she had left him. "Any change?"

Waggs shook his head. "No, but his chart looks good."

The room was big and airy with its own private bathroom and a couch which had become her bed the last few days. She knew she was never alone; one of the team was always here or in the hallway.

"How is the investigation going? Do we know if anyone else was involved?"

It still sickened her that a man her family trusted would try and kill her, but at least Mitch had killed him. It should make her a monster, but she had no remorse over his death, for being glad he was dead. She should but she simply could not. As far as she was concerned, he deserved to rot in hell.

"We're checking it all out now. Lopez has checked all his bank accounts, and it seems whatever made him do it wasn't money. We're delving into his private life now. From what we know he never married, but Lopez is digging. Everyone else is in the clear. Scott traces back to Mustafa, so does Hassan. Your father and brother are also clearing house, they fired half of the security team and have Zack consulting to employ new ones."

"Oh, wow, I did not know that." Taamira pursed her lips. "Are we sure Mustafa did not act alone?"

"We don't think so," Waggs added.

Her sharp gaze turned to him. "Why?"

"We found a burner phone he was using with texts and calls to only one number, which is also a burner. The texts suggest that person is calling the shots."

"Once we have them, this will be over for you, Princess," Mitch added.

"We should get going. Call us if you need anything," Pax said as she leaned to press a kiss to her cheek.

"I will."

Waggs winked at her. "Mitch and I will be outside in the hallway if you need anything."

"Thank you."

As they all filed out, Taamira wondered how she had lived so long without these people in her life.

———

He could hear muffled conversation coming at him as if through a cloud of cotton wool. A soft hand landed on his arm, warming his cold skin and he wanted to reach out for her, instantly knowing it was Taamira, but he couldn't seem to form the words or move his hands.

He heard other voices too, but all he could see was darkness surrounding him in a warm fog. He tried to remember what had happened, why he was there and yet couldn't fully grasp the memory. All he could remember was pain and shouting and then he saw Ambrose. His friend's face hovered just out of reach and couldn't figure out which way to turn.

"Go back, brother."

"I miss you, my friend."

"And I you, but it isn't time. You still have lots of living to do."

"I'm sorry I let you down."

Liam let the devastation of failure gouge pain through his body all over again, the guilt of not being there for his friend almost crippling him.

Ambrose chuckled and shook his head. "Why do you take on the troubles of the world as if they are your own? You couldn't have known what was going to happen that day."

"I should've been where I said I'd be, and then you'd still be alive."

"But then you may not have met Taamira. She needs you, Liam. She loves you as Gail loved me, like she still loves me."

"Gail hates me."

"Gail loves you, but she was hurting. My son needs his uncle, and the woman I love needs to know it's okay to move on. She needs you to tell her it's okay."

"How do I stop missing you? It's as if my arm has been torn off and I only have half of me left."

"Forgive yourself, brother, because I forgive you, my friend. Not for letting me down, because you didn't, but because you let yourself down. Go live a good life, make lots of babies with your princess and keep an eye on my son. Make sure he knows how much I loved him."

Ambrose was growing fainter and Liam wanted to reach out to him but as he did, Taamira's sweet voice became louder, her face hovering over him as he blinked his eyes. His friend was gone but the woman he loved with every breath in his body was smiling down at him with tears in her eyes.

"You came back to me."

Liam had enough energy to smile before sleep pulled him back under.

CHAPTER TWENTY-EIGHT

Taamira could not stop smiling as she hit the call button for the nurse. Instantly Waggs and Mitch rushed in with a nurse not far behind them. Looks of alarm were on their faces until they saw her smile.

"He opened his eyes."

Tears were streaming down her face, but she didn't care. Liam had opened his eyes and looked at her; he had known her. Her hand remained in his, and she felt the strength of it as he gripped hers back for the first time.

"That's wonderful," the nurse said cheerfully as she began to do some checks on Liam as Waggs hovered.

She liked that he did, knowing he would explain it all to her as he had been this entire time. His training as a medic affording him the knowledge she wished she had.

"I'll get the doctor to check him out, but it seems he's starting to come around properly. The pump just administered another dose of pain medication so that probably knocked him out again."

The nurse walked away, and she turned to Waggs, who was

smiling at her. "This is good news, Princess." He hugged her, and she didn't fight the smile and the relief that flooded her body.

The doctor came in moments later and did the same checks the nurse had done as well as a few others. "Mr Hayes seems to be responding to stimulus. We will lower his pain medication a little and see if that helps him to come around fully. We are most definitely on the right track now." He adjusted the drip slightly and fiddled with the pump, administering pain relief, and then noted it in his chart.

Once everyone had left again and feeling happier than she had since this whole nightmare began, she curled up on the couch close to the window, letting the autumn sun warm her face.

Lifting her mobile phone from her bag, she sent a text to her father to let him know Liam was improving. He responded straight away, telling her how pleased he was and that he would continue to pray for them both. Taamira also asked he pass the message on to Abdul which he agreed to do.

She glanced across the room at the man she loved and knew in her heart it would all be okay now. No matter what they faced, as long as they had each other it would be okay. That didn't detract from the love she had for her new friends, but it was different. Without Liam, she couldn't breathe, without her friends, she was sad beyond belief, but Liam was her heart.

Picking up his phone, which the nurses had given her when they collected all his belongings, she ran her finger over the face of it. He had no family; his parents were alive, but he hadn't spoken to them in years. She hesitated over the name of one contact before she made a decision and hit dial.

Taamira must have dozed off for a few minutes after putting in the call she hoped wasn't a mistake. Her phone buzzed again, and she read the text, surprised it was from her sister-in-law.

Fawzaana: Can we talk? I could come to the hospital so you don't have to leave Liam alone."

· · ·

Taamira gave it a moment's thought before she replied.

Taamira: Yes, You can do that. Come to the room and we can speak.
What is it about?"
    Fawzaana: I want to talk about Abdul, he misses you.

Taamira was intrigued. She and Fawzaana had never been close,
but for her brother, she would see what the woman wanted. Mitch
and Waggs would be close so she would be safe.

Taamira: Come to the hospital in thirty minutes, and I will see you.

Taamira wasn't usually so demanding, but she knew it was best
for this woman to know who was higher up the pecking order or she
would lord it over her. She was done being a doormat to that spiteful
person.
    Taamira stood and let Waggs and Mitch know to let Fawzaana
in. She could see they didn't like it but went along with her
request.

Thirty minutes later, Fawzaana swept into the room, casting her
eye around as she did, before her eyes came to rest on Liam in the
bed. He was still sleeping, but it was a lighter sleep now.
    Waggs tilted his head to her. "We're just outside the door if you
need us."
    "Thank you, Waggs." She smiled back before she greeted her
sister-in-law. "Fawzaana, would you like to sit?"

Mitch and Waggs had forced her guard to wait outside, and she looked smaller without them around her.

"No, I wish to stand."

Still a raging bitch then.

Taamira went to stand the other side of the bed, her hand reaching for Liam's automatically. She saw the sneer on Fawzaana's face as she looked at them.

The woman looked regal in an olive-green kaftan with bronze embroidery at the edges. A scarf of olive green covered her head, and the loose trousers she wore were in the same bronze as the stitching fell to her feet where she wore silk pumps. By contrast, Taamira wore pale jeans and one of Liam's t-shirts, with flat pumps on her feet.

"What did you wish to talk about?" Taamira saw no point with pleasantries.

Fawzaana moved closer to the bed, her hands hidden in the folds of her sleeves and Taamira's guard rose, her senses tingling at the way Fawzaana was looking at her. The woman kept looking at Liam in the bed and it was unnerving her, she needed to get Fawzaana's attention back on her.

"Fawzaana, speak, or I will call Waggs to escort you out."

Fawzaana glanced up at her at the same time she withdrew a deadly looking knife from her sleeve. "I don't think you will, or Liam will not survive the next attack."

Taamira gripped Liam's hand, her other coming up towards Fawzaana. "What are you doing?"

Suddenly things began to make sense, the inside job, the way the person had such close access to her nieces.

"If you want something done, do it yourself. Isn't that the saying? I want you to die, but first, you will watch him die like I had to watch my love die."

"You and Mustafa?"

Fawzaana laughed, but it was hollow and empty. "I have loved him since the day we met, but I had to marry Abdul. It was what my family decreed, and a good Eyan woman does not go against her family. Yet, you could always do as you pleased. The Crown Princess had different rules than the rest of us."

"Why did you not tell your family? Abdul would not have forced it if he had known."

Fawzaana looked at her as her hand inched closer to Liam's side, where his heart beat, the hatred on her face turning her features ugly. "Silly girl, you do not say no to a future king. Mustafa had it all planned, we would run away, but then I got pregnant with Najwa, and our plans changed! Then Mamina came along. Your stupid father underestimated me, but when you started to rebel, we saw a way to destabilise the family."

Taamira fought the snarl at the hate-filled words aimed at her father. "Is Mustafa Najwa and Mamina's father?"

"Of course he isn't. I am not a fool. I needed my daughters to have royal blood for my plan to work."

"What was the plan?" Taamira asked as Liam's fingers flexed in hers.

He was awake but staying still as if he still slept. Taamira feared he would do something to save her and get himself killed for real this time.

"To dishonour you. We paid the men on the island to kidnap you, and when your father authorised the ransom, Abdul gave his trusted guard the order. Unfortunately, it did not translate, but then those men saved you."

"How would dishonouring me help you?" Taamira swallowed the bile that another woman could order that sort of attack on a sister.

"It would distance you even further from the family and make Abdul more malleable. He has always been easy to manipulate, but you were his adored sister, and everything came back to you. There were a number of times I had to convince him to do things a certain way instead of following what you would want."

"I still do not understand. How did that help you and Mustafa?" The knife was resting against Liam's ribcage now, the vicious-looking blade touching his skin.

"With you dead, the King would have a nasty heart attack. We would all mourn then a few months later, a tragic accident would befall Abdul, leaving his underage daughter the sole heir to the Eyan throne."

"Meaning you would be Queen Regent until she was of age."

"Now you understand, but you killed the man I love, and now I must do the same to you."

"You will never get away with this. Men are outside the door, if you hurt Liam they will come running."

"None of it matters anymore. I would rather die than live without him."

"Fawzaana, do not say that. What about Najwa and Mamina? They need you."

"No, they do not, they always favoured their father over me."

Taamira couldn't deny that because it was true.

"Say goodbye."

Fawzaana moved suddenly, and Taamira screamed and dove across the bed, but Liam had grabbed hold of Fawzaana's wrist in a lethal grip, twisting it so the knife clattered to the ground.

Mitch and Waggs burst through the door and subdued a screaming Fawzaana, who held her mangled wrist to her chest.

"Liam, are you okay? Did she hurt you?" Her hands were all over his body, looking for injury as he groaned.

His eyes flashed to hers and he grinned. "I'm fine, but you need to get your sweet little hands off me before I embarrass us both."

Taamira frowned and looked at him as she backed up, but he snagged her hand in his bringing her close. "Your touch drives me crazy," he said looking at his crotch purposefully as Mitch chuckled and dragged Fawzaana towards the door.

Taamira smiled and dropped a pineapple lip balm flavoured kiss to his lips. "I love you."

"Back at ya, Princess."

———

His recovery had not been as quick as he had envisaged, but five days after he'd woken, he'd been allowed to travel home. That had been three weeks ago, and he was already stronger. He had a strict regimen to follow, and near-daily visits from Waggs which he knew were as much for Taamira's benefit as his. His woman fussed over him constantly; he understood it and figured he would be the same in her position.

It turned out they hadn't created a baby that day and the news had been a blow that he'd not expected, but it had cemented his feelings for Taamira. He loved her so much it hurt, and it terrified him because the thought of losing her made him shake with fear.

Whether his chat with his dead friend had actually happened or had been a result of the drugs, he didn't know, but the end result was the same. He needed to put his grief to the back of his mind. He would never stop missing Ambrose, but he was alive, and he needed to live life for both of them.

He discovered Laverne and Astrid had flown to Eyan while he was unconscious and questioned the household staff at the Palace about Mustafa, and had called Jack, who had been in the middle of calling Mitch when Fawzaana had attempted to stab him. That Laverne and Astrid had done that off their own back to help a friend meant they would have his gratitude for the rest of his days.

He curled his arm around Taamira as they lay on the couch, watching the second season of Hawaii Five-o, her body lying in the space in front of him, his arms around her.

"Do you need any pain killers?" Taamira went to move, and he tightened his hold.

"No."

"Food? Drink? I can make you something?"

"All I need is you right here in my arms."

Taamira smiled and turned towards him, the tv show forgotten. "I can do that."

"Although..."

She went to move, and he held her again, a twitch on his lips.

"What?"

"I wouldn't mind a walk outside to see Digby."

He watched her eyes light up at the sound of the donkey's name.

She scrambled up and held her hands to him. He stood with only a tiny bit of pain, feeling a hundred times better than he had. He had waited as long as he could, but he needed this to happen today.

With their hands entwined they walked towards Digby. The animal trotted over to them and he saw Pax had done as he'd asked.

Taamira smiled when she saw the bow around his neck, her eyes flitting to his in question. "What is all this?"

She let his hand go and grabbed the donkey's collar, twisting it to see the note attached. When she turned around, she gasped as he sank to one knee, her hands flying to her mouth.

Liam took her hand in his, pulling it from her face. "Taamira, you changed my life from the second I met you, filling every second with life and joy that I never thought I deserved. You have shown me how to live, how to be a better person, and I want to spend the rest of my life loving you, building a family with you and growing old with you. Will you please marry me, treacle?"

Taamira sank to her knees, throwing her arms around him as she nodded. "Yes, I'll marry you."

Liam kissed her then, pouring every ounce of the love he had for her into it. Digby nudged him with his nose, and they broke apart laughing.

"Think we should maybe take this to the bedroom?" He smiled as he stood and rubbed the animal's snout.

"Are you well enough for that?"

Liam laughed and swung her into his arms as she gasped. "I've never felt better."

"Well, let's get started on the rest of our lives."

EPILOGUE

STANDING at the altar in a black tuxedo, Liam looked out at the friends and family in the pews as he waited for the love of his life to finally become his wife. He had never thought he'd be so blessed, but he was.

Alex stood beside him as his best man, Blake, Reid, and Jack as his ushers, the rest of his brothers watching, including the Fortis team and their wives and children. Some with very pregnant partners, the Fortis family was expanding yet again.

He wondered how long it would be before he and Taamira started a family. He wanted a little time alone, but he couldn't wait for her to have his child. His eyes caught on a very special lady in the pew behind Prince Abdul.

Gail grinned at him as she sat with her new man, a good man who Liam liked very much. He would never be Ambrose, but she was happy. They'd had a good talk after his attack and put the past behind them. He loved having Natai in his life again, and Taamira and Gail had hit it off wonderfully.

His eyes moved to Prince Abdul. The man had taken a blow learning of his wife's crimes and lies but as the months had gone on,

Taamira said she had begun to see the brother she had played hide and seek with emerging from the remains.

Fawzaana had been sent back to Eyan where she had faced charges of treason and attempted murder. She was now serving a life sentence in the jail at Eyan. Her daughters had cut her from their lives, and Taamira and Callie had been instrumental in finding them the support they needed to deal with that.

The music began, and Liam's eyes moved to the top of the aisle. His smile split his face when he saw Natai walking down the aisle with a pillow in his hands. He smiled at Liam and abandoned the slow walk for a little jog. Liam crouched down and caught him.

"Uncle Liam, I did it, and I never dropped the rings."

Liam chuckled, along with those closest to them who'd overheard Natai's words. "Good job, buddy. Can you hand them to Alex for me?"

Natai nodded and Alex took his hand.

Pax and Evelyn were next, looking gorgeous in burgundy dresses in a delicate lace, followed by Callie, Laverne, and Astrid and finally Najwa and Mamina, all looking equally stunning in the same gowns. The cream flowers complimenting the entire wedding ensemble.

His breath caught when he saw his wife-to-be with her father at the top by the church doors. He had wanted to turn around, but couldn't do it, he needed to see her.

King Saud had given his blessing to Liam before the proposal. The note Digby had around his neck contained the royal decree of approval. Not that it would have stopped Liam, but he had wanted it for Taamira, to help mend the broken fences of the relationship with her family.

The floor-length gown of rich cream was embroidered all over with gold silk thread flowers, the deep vee neck daring but the flesh coloured sleeves and netting giving it a little modesty. She carried dark red flowers native to her beloved Eyan, a tiara of gold, ruby, and diamonds on her regal head.

It was her smile that was the most radiant he had ever seen it. As she stopped beside him, her father handed her over with a slight bow before taking his seat in the front beside his son.

"I am so excited," she murmured.

"You look beyond beautiful."

Taamira smiled. "You look very dashing too. I am so lucky to have found you."

"You didn't find me, treacle, fate dictated you were mine the day you were born."

Her face went soft and they turned to the priest who would marry them.

The service was a blur, but he tried to take in every single second of their wedding day. Noting the way she looked as she spoke with their friends, wanting to treasure this day so that when he was old, he could reminisce about the day the cockney married a princess.

"You look happy."

He turned to catch Gail smiling at him. "I am. Never thought I'd be this happy, but she is my world."

"I'm happy for you, Liam, and Ambrose would be as well."

Liam put his arm around Gail. "I know he would. I miss him every day."

"Me too, but he would want us to live life to the full as he had."

"Yes, he would, and I finally remembered that with the help of Taamira."

Gail raised up and kissed his cheek. "Be happy, my friend."

"You too."

He watched Gail walk away with her new man, Toby, and turned to catch Taamira watching him. He crooked his finger at her, and she grinned as she walked towards him.

"You called?" she said with a smile.

"I missed my wife."

"I love hearing you say that."

"Me too. Want to dance or get some air?"

"Air, please."

He slid his arm around her waist and walked with her to the

French doors of the 18th-century castle where they were holding the reception, the service having been at the small church on the grounds, and away from the prying eyes of the press, who had taken Taamira into their hearts.

They walked to the edge of the patio, and he took her in his arms, swaying gently as the evening light faded.

"This has been the happiest day of my life," Liam said as he twirled her to the music playing softly in the background.

"Mine, too. But I know each and every day with you gets better and better. So, you know what you said about starting a family?" Taamira said as he twirled her again before bringing her back to his body.

"Yes."

"How would you feel about starting it eight months from today?"

Liam went stock still as his eyes pricked with emotion. His hand went to her belly as he dropped his gaze. "Are you seriously saying what I think you are?"

Taamira nodded, tears in her own eyes. "Yes, I took the test this morning."

"Every time I think my life can't get better you give me more beauty to be grateful for."

Her hands curled in the hair at his neck as she raised up her lips hovering inches from his. "I want to spend my life making you happy that you saved me."

"Treacle, you have that wrong, you saved me."

"I guess we saved each other then."

"I guess we did."

That was the story he would tell his children as they grew older, how the cockney saved the princess, and the princess saved him right back.

SNEAK PEAK: MITCH

Mitchel Quinn and Autumn Roberts

Mitch hooked his thumbs in the loops of his pockets as he looked up at the old building in need of a little TLC. Glancing sideways, he nodded up toward the roofline as he spoke to his friend, Nate. "What would a new roof set me back?"

Nate owned a similar property three doors away and had completely renovated it into the large family home it was now.

Nate shoved his hand in his pockets as he stepped back to look up at the broken roof tiles. "Around ten to fifteen grand, I'd say."

Nate worked for Fortis Security, a company Eidolon did a lot of work with, and the teams got on well and socialised together a fair bit too. Hereford was not a vast metropolis, so it was expected they would run in similar circles, but it was the fact he and Nate were both snipers that made the two of them tight.

Mitch whistled thinking of his bank balance, trying to do some quick calculations in his head. "That's a decent chunk of change."

Nate nodded. "It is but these properties are solid. It's an investment in the long run."

Mitch looked up again at the sprawling Victorian home that spanned three floors. It had already been split into four separate flats by the previous owner. That meant he could rent three of them out for extra income.

He'd been working for Eidolon for a few years now and was happy there. Hereford was home now, and he wanted to put down some roots, invest in his future, and as Nate's father David constantly reminded him, bricks and mortar were always a good investment long term.

Glancing at the windows which would need replacing, he could see how the property could swallow money if he let it but as Mitch stared silently, he could also the potential.

"Be nice when it's done up. Most of the work is cosmetic apart from the roof and windows."

"Make a nice family home one day too." Nate chuckled.

Mitch held up his hands with a raised eyebrow, a grin on his lips. "Hey steady on, I'm too young for all that."

"Yeah, whatever, gramps. I need to get back. Skye has to deliver a cake to a bride at the Left Bank and I need to watch Nancy and Noah." Nate held up a hand as he walked up the street.

That was the biggest difference between the two friends. Nate was a devoted family man and Mitch at forty-five was a dedicated bachelor.

It wasn't that he wanted to be, or that he played the field the way he used to in his younger days, just that it had never happened. He'd seen far too many marriages fail in his time as a member of SO19, the Firearms division of the London Metropolitan Police Department. So many relationships had crumbled from the pressures of the job, and he had no intention of forcing one just to satisfy convention.

He would rather wait until he could have what Alex, Blake, Reid, and now Liam had with their women. If that meant it didn't happen, he'd be okay with what he had.

Mitch strolled around to the back of the property for one last look before he made his decision. Later that day, his offer on the property was accepted.

Six months later, Mitch was living in one of the top floor flats. Decker had rented one of the ground floor ones, and Bebe, one of the Zenobi girls, had the other ground floor flat. It suited him having tenants he knew, especially since he'd spent more cash doing it up than he'd intended. That's why the last apartment on the top floor opposite his own was up for rental through an agency. He had little worry he'd end up with a bad tenant with all the hoops people had to jump through and especially with Will, the owner of Eidolon and tech genius, offering to run background checks on them first.

His phone rang as he was walking into a meeting with the team and he quickly answered it, stepping aside as Waggs walked past him and into the large conference room. "Yep."

"Mr Quinn, this is Melissa from the letting agency. We have a potential tenant for you."

"Great."

"But they can only view the property after hours."

"And?" He moved his hand in a wrap this up gesture even though she couldn't see him.

"We were wondering if you could show them around?"

Mitch sighed, he had no time for this, but he would be around so he guessed it wouldn't be too much of an imposition. "Yeah, sure, what time?"

"Is eight tonight too late?"

"Nah, that's fine."

"Thank you. I'll let Miss Roberts know."

Mitch hung up and walked into the conference room where everyone was waiting. He clapped Liam on the shoulder as he took the seat next to him. "How are you feeling?"

"Pucker mate."

Liam insisted on using cockney words to irritate the rest of the team who barely understood them half the time, although they seemed to be learning quick enough.

Mitch nodded glad to see his friend back on rotation and fighting fit again.

Jack, their boss, banged the table with one hand. "Listen up. We have a few things to cover."

The room began to silence as all of the men focused on the job, first and foremost.

Firstly, we had word from the palace that the Queen wants to do a tour of the commonwealth next year." Jack flipped a pencil end over end as he spoke. "That means we're up. We need to plan it, visit locations, and prep. Her usual security will continue with the day to day stuff, but this is where we shine, gentleman. We need this contract if you want to keep making money."

"What about the threat inside the palace? Has Gunner given us anything useful?" Decker leaned back in his chair the coolest cucumber in the room, and the most well-dressed. He lived in a suit while the rest of them wore, jeans, combats, or training gear. Perhaps it was because as the profiler, his brain was his biggest weapon, whereas they were more the brawn."

"He's meeting me in two days and says he might have a name for us by then." Jack sat forward. "Any questions?"

"You got any closer to hiring a dog unit?"

Blake was the one with the most experience in personal protection, having had close contact with the Queen long before they got this contract. He was all in favour of having a K9 unit for the teams. Mitch had to say he agreed, it worked for Fortis well and was the only place they had a real gap in capabilities.

"I'm interviewing candidates with Alex and Decker on Friday."

"What about admin and stuff? I'm sick of getting stuck with that shit," Lopez whined.

Mitch threw a ball of paper at his head. "Stop whining, you big baby."

Lopez lobbed it back. "You try doing it and see how you like it."

"Can't, they need my exceptional skill in the field, nerd boy."

"Fuck off, grandad."

Mitch laughed at the dig, knowing it was a joke. As the oldest member of the team he frequently got called gramps and grandad—it didn't bother him in the slightest.

"When did forty become old?"

"When did it stop?" Lopez countered, and the guys cracked up as did he.

"Touché."

This camaraderie was why he loved this team; they laughed, they joked, but when it mattered, they would take a bullet to save one another. It was a similar feeling to the one he'd had long ago when he grew up surrounded by his gang, except the current one was highly trained and mostly legal.

Until Eidolon, he'd missed that element of belonging that being part of a crew had given him. It was the only part he did miss though. The rest had been too high a price to pay for his best friend's life.

Walking away from the gangs, getting out of South London had literally saved his own life. It was something he would be forever grateful for, and his mum was the woman he would always have to thank for it. As a single mum since his dad's death, she had worked her fingers to the bone to keep a roof over their heads, and not once had he gone without. But ultimately, it was her grit, her strength to drag him bodily to another area and away from the people who would have cost him his life had he stayed, that was the thing he was most grateful for.

Jack leaned forward on the table catching everyone's attention, holding a room with his authority in such a way nobody realised it half the time. "Well, Lopez you'll be happy to hear that I've looked at the budget and hired an office admin."

"Thank fuck for that. Tell me she's pretty, with long legs...."

"She is off fucking limits. Aubrey will have my balls if you touch her sister, and anyway, I'm not having you pricks hitting on the office staff and costing me a fortune in legal fees when she sues us."

"Madison? Are you fucking kidding me?" Lopez threw his pen down on the desk, shaking his head. Madison was a handful to say the least. The team had already saved her from a Colombian drug lord.

"It's a favour for Aubrey."

Nobody responded to that, because everyone loved Aubrey, Will's girlfriend, and a local police detective.

"I'm also hiring someone to co-ordinate logistics for us. Pax has very kindly agreed to help me find someone."

"Pax should come work for us. She'd be awesome." Reid looked at Blake with a raised brow.

"Not going to happen, my friend, she's loyal to Roz. Plus, we'd probably kill each other."

Reid laughed. "True dat."

Pax was the most efficient woman Mitch had ever met, and she would be a massive asset to the team, but he had to respect her loyalty to Zenobi.

Jack stood from his chair, leaning his hands on the table. "Well if that's all, we can meet here next Monday and go through a detailed list of jobs when I've met with the Palace."

"Need someone with you?" Mitch asked, not liking the idea of Jack going into that alone when they knew a threat to the team originated there.

"Blake is coming with me, but a second set of eyes would be good."

Mitch nodded, and everyone stood as the meeting wrapped up. Mitch looked at his watch and figured he had time for a workout before he met the prospective tenant.

That turned out to be longer than expected when he got into sparring matched with Waggs and Reid, and then Alex joined them. Before he knew what had happened, it was seven-thirty.

"Fuck, I need to be somewhere."

Throwing his gloves in his bag, he rushed through a shower and shoved his jeans, navy t-shirt and boots on before jumping in his car and driving the fifteen minutes home.

Pulling up, he noticed a rusted out Ford Focus parked on the road outside his house and cussed again. He hated being late for anything.

Throwing his bag over his shoulder, he stepped through the front gate and came face to butt with the sweetest ass he had ever seen, and Mitch had seen his fair share. A sexy woman with long black hair in braids was bending over pulling weeds from his garden.

"You here to see the flat or did I contract a gardener and forget about it?"

The woman instantly turned and flashed him a questioning smile. Forget the ass, her face was even better, with a regal, oval-shaped face, a warm rose gold skin tone, and lush, full lips meant for kissing. The woman tilted her head to look up at him with eyes the colour of autumn leaves, the longest lashes he'd ever seen sweeping over high cheekbones. Her long black hair was held back from her face in a knot, the rest skimming almost to her waist as she moved toward him, hand outstretched.

"Mr Quinn, I'm Autumn Roberts." She waved a hand behind her. "Sorry about that, I couldn't help myself. Gardening is a bit of a passion of mine."

"Mitch."

She frowned adorably, her hands rubbing together to get the soil off them, and he fought not to grin like an idiot. "Sorry?"

"My name is Mitch."

"Oh, I see."

He regarded her taking in the whole package and found himself intrigued. This woman was beautiful and friendly, a good start.

"Can I see the property?"

Mitch jumped. "Oh yeah, sure." He moved toward the door feeling like a knobend for staring at the poor woman.

He led her to the stairs and looked back at her as she looked around. "It's on the top floor."

He opened the door and let her go in first, wanting another look at her rear end to see if his assessment had been spot on the first time. Yes, it definitely had, her curves filled out those jeans perfectly.

Shaking his head, he walked to towards the kitchen area. "It's fitted out with new units and appliances. Carpets and laminate are also new, so is the bathroom suite and windows."

Autumn walked to the window and looked out at the long garden. "Do you allow children? The agent wasn't sure."

"As long as they're housetrained and not gonna keep everyone up all night." He'd hoped to elicit a smile from her wanting to see how she looked with a full grin on her stunning face.

"Maggie is only five months old, so not exactly." Her face was motionless as she watched him, a caution about her he didn't understand but for some strange reason wanted to.

"It was a joke, Miss Roberts. Kids are fine."

She offered him another of her shy smiles and then dipped her head. "When can I move in?"

Mitch moved to stand beside her and noticed the scent of honeysuckle surrounded her. It was sweet and suited her and made his dick jump with interest.

"As soon as your references and DBS check come back clear."

Her face dropped again, and she nodded but wouldn't meet his eyes. "Okay."

"You gonna take it?"

"Yeah, I think I am."

Mitch grinned at her, shoving his hands in his pockets, to keep from the acting on the sudden urge to reach for her.

He had the distinct impression that Miss Roberts was going to make his life very interesting.

For the first time in a long time, he was excited by a woman, whether that would be a good thing or a bad one was anyone's guess.

Order Mitch Now

BOOKS BY MADDIE WADE

Fortis Security

Healing Danger (Dane and Lauren)

Stolen Dreams (Nate and Skye)

Love Divided (Jace and Lucy)

Secret Redemption (Zack and Ava)

Broken Butterfly (Zin and Celeste)

Arctic Fire (Kanan and Roz)

Phoenix Rising (Daniel and Megan)

Nate & Skye Wedding Novella

Digital Desire (Will and Aubrey)

Paradise Ties: A Fortis Wedding Novella (Jace and Lucy & Dane and Lauren)

Wounded Hearts (Drew and Mara)

Scarred Sunrise (Smithy and Lizzie)

Zin and Celeste: A Fortis Family Christmas

Fortis Boxset 1 (Books 1-3)

Fortis Boxset 2 (Books 4-7.5

————

Eidolon

Alex

Blake

Reid

Liam

Mitch

Gunner

Waggs

Jack

Lopez

———

Alliance Agency Series (co-written with India Kells)
Deadly Alliance

Knight Watch

Hidden Obsession

Lethal Justice

Innocent Target

———

Ryoshi Delta (part of Susan Stoker's Police and Fire: Operation Alpha World)
Condor's Vow

Sandstorm's Promise

Hawk's Honor

Omega's Oath

———

Tightrope Duet
Tightrope One

Tightrope Two

ABOUT THE AUTHOR

Contact Me

If stalking an author is your thing and I sure hope it is then here are the links to my social media pages.

If you prefer your stalking to be more intimate, then my group Maddie's Minxes will welcome you with open arms.

General Email: info.maddiewade@gmail.com
Email: maddie@maddiewadeauthor.co.uk
Website: http://www.maddiewadeauthor.co.uk
Facebook page: https://www.facebook.com/maddieuk/
Facebook group: https://www.facebook.com/groups/5463250355578882/
Amazon Author page: amazon.com/author/maddiewade
Goodreads: https://www.goodreads.com/author/show/14854265.Maddie_Wade
Bookbub: https://partners.bookbub.com/authors/3711690/edit
Twitter: @mwadeauthor
Pinterest: @maddie_wade
Instagram: Maddie Author

Printed in Great Britain
by Amazon

37818965R00126